HINDSIGHT

Hindsight

and Other Stories

Joan Corwin

Published by Serving House Books
Lawrence Landing Company
Raleigh, North Carolina 27609
United States of America
www.servinghousebooks.com

Serving House Books is a proud member of

Independent Book Publishers Association
 and
Community of Literary Magazines and Presses

Paperback ISBN: 978-1-947175-68-6

Library of Congress Control Number:
 2025933389

SERVING HOUSE BOOKS

in memory of Melody

we were never lost;

we were exactly where we wanted to be

CONTENTS

POINT MAN

I take point with these guys on an interstate job hitting a truckload of electronics, really good stuff, the kind with German names you never heard of—but hard to move. I'd rather hit a semi full of iPods, easy to dispose of and tough to trace. So I'm nervous about the game because the goods are too shine. Plus, it's for that prick Scissors. But I need the work, and besides, the guys on the team—Nick's team—are pros. And I'm their point man.

You want somebody quiet on point, somebody who can listen. I'm a good listener. I'm the only one ever listens to the frogs, for instance. Those little frogs, the kind that get quiet as soon as they sense someone near, like thousands of tiny point men. Listening to the frogs got me where I am today.

It was a couple years back, summer, a target out in the sticks. I was on another team, not point man, just a hump. Someone dimed us out, so we heard later, and there was a flock of uniforms, local Barneys, lying in wait for us. They had to start whispering or squirming around, making some kind of noise, because before we even got close, all the frogs stopped chirping. I was the only one who noticed. I moved to the front and signaled the team. We backed off real quiet, got in our rides and slipped away. Nick heard how this went down, and the next thing

I know I got a permanent gig as point man with his team.

This time, the team is me and Nick and Bernie and Mickey. The only actor we don't know is the rig driver, but he comes with good credentials and he's got a fake trucker's ID. He's a cross-roader, always on the move from town to town, con to con. A floater like this, sometimes he's the best guy for the job, but you have to be able to trust him, because when the hustle's done, he is gone. The deal is, we pay him half up front and he leaves the trailer for us at the drop spot, drives the cab one state over and dumps that at a rest stop, where we have a car and the other half of the cash waiting for him.

It's a good spot, where we break open the trailer. It's out-of-the-way, secluded, set back in the woods. Not a place you come on if you're not looking for it it. We know the trailer will still be there when we arrive, because once you back eighteen wheels down that dirt drive, you're inclined to leave the load behind when you go.

As point, I'm supposed to be the first to the trailer and the last in. We've got an old Lincoln Town Car and a van, so we have room to transport a decent-size score without drawing attention, and we park far enough that I can suss the scene before calling the others in. The trailer is exactly where it should be, and the cab is gone.

This night, it's a beautiful night. The sky is full of stars. It's not easy taking point under a sky like that. You don't want to get distracted when you're on point. But this spot is so secure that I can look up for a second or two without worrying about getting jumped. Besides, you can hear those little frogs chirping all over the place.

I think I'm moving without a sound, gliding almost, but I notice the chirps go out one after the other when I pass, like I'm carrying this shell of quiet with me. Once I reach the container, I see the padlock's swinging free, which means the driver helped himself before he left, and this makes me stop and listen to the dark. When I'm convinced we are alone, I pull the doors and wave everyone to come in. But the stench hits me and I gag. The others see me double over and out comes the hardware. (I don't carry a gun—it's the best way I know to get killed on a lick.) I guess they figure we've been suckered, that someone inside the trailer took me down when I opened it, though by this time the smell's got to make an impression, and why they think something dead long enough to stink like that is in any condition to fight, I don't know.

I can hardly breathe, but I shine my flashlight into the trailer, holding it away from my body so I'm not a target in the dark. And I can't believe what I see. By now it's clear there's nobody in that trailer that we have to worry about, so the other guys close in, one hand over nose and mouth, the other aiming a flashlight. Our four beams light up the load, so then I have to believe it.

The trailer is full of little cages, floor to ceiling, and in them are little hairy heaps. They're not moving, but the threads of light cross each other and make the shadows shrink and stretch and dodge, picking up a face here, a tail there, a little hairy arm hanging through the bars. They're monkeys, dead monkeys. Scores of them, each with its own little cage.

I never liked monkeys. People, girls mostly, think they're cute, but they're too human for me. They look like what people would look like if all the good was freeze-dried out of them—little, shriveled, hairy pieces of evil.

"Fuck! Fuck me!" Mickey's spitting, he's so angry. "It's the wrong rig!"

"How the fuck did this happen?" Bernie screams in that high voice he has. "Who the fuck was our intel?"

"Guy in the trucking company," says Nick. He's cool like always. When I try to put Nick's cool into context, to account for it, I imagine a shooting range somewhere with all the targets' heads blown off, or a punching bag leaking sawdust from a thousand holes. "It happens," he says, pulling out his cigarettes. "Last minute change or something." He doesn't believe this. He knows the driver is supposed to check the load before he hits the road, so either our driver didn't do his job, or we've been set up.

That last idea strikes us all at the same time and we spin around expecting to get wasted or collared. The night is quiet, except for those little frogs, which start up again like they've got us figured, like we're no threat.

"So how'd they die?" asks Bernie. He's snapping his fingers like he does when he's nervous, and even in gloves, they sound like shots. I've taped his fingers together sometimes when I know the job is going to involve serious stealth. His mouth is another issue. "How? How'd they die?" The rest of us look at each other and shrug. But there's no such thing as a rhetorical question with Bernie. Somebody has to answer, or he'll never stop.

"Experiments probably," grunts Mickey. "You know, like in labs where they test stuff on animals."

I'm scanning the labels on the cages now with my light, and these monkeys aren't test monkeys. They're for pet stores back East. But they're all dead—at least, all but one. Not that it's making any noise. It's just that when the guys turn away from the doors, I make a sweep, one last sweep, and all the other little shiny eyes must be closed because it's only in this one cage that the beam picks them up, two tiny beads of light, looking right at me. We almost missed it, almost shut it back up in there alive. I break out in a sweat when I think about that.

"Wait a minute," I say, though the instant I do, I feel like I just sawed through the wrong end of a tree limb I'm sitting on. "Wait a minute. That one's alive." I can sense the guys sending each other signals behind my back, and there is a chance that they'll shut the doors on me when I go for the monkey. But I have to go in. I saw its eyes looking right at me. I saw its eyes, and it saw me.

My sister had that look. She had the look. I had the ears. I could hear when the old man reached the fork at Philly's Mill more than a mile from home. I'd take the flashlight, not the broken one he beat me with, the working one that I hid in the pantry in the crockpot we never used. And a sleeping bag. And I'd leave. My sister'd just look at me. Twenty-three years later, I'm point man for Nick's team, and there's that look again.

I feel their eyes on my back when I climb into the trailer, but they don't shut me in. Maybe they're afraid one of them will have to wax me first so that no one finds the trailer with me alive in it. Maybe each guy is waiting for the others to do it. Maybe this is why they don't leave me to die with the monkey, among monkeys. Or maybe they're just good guys, I don't know. I lost perspective on that over the years.

"Look, Pete," says Mickey, "it's just a monkey and . . . Jesus, it stinks!" he adds when I bring the cage out, the little animal in there just sitting, not moving, staring at us, the loss of the other monkeys sitting so heavy on it, it's like a swallow that won't go down. And I know it stinks, and I know it's a monkey, which is a thing I hate, but there's something about the way it studies us, one at a time, that makes even Mickey and Bernie stop grumbling and look at their feet.

The only one that matters, though, is Nick, and I glance over to where he's lighting his cigarette. He's got his hands cupped so I can't see his face.

"I'll take care of it," I say, and there is a crash in my ears like the Seal of Doom. But it's just Mickey closing the back of the trailer.

No one will ride in the Town Car with me and the monkey because of the smell. I shrug, put the monkey in back and climb into the driver's seat, even though I am not one of our drivers—point men never are. But no one says anything. They just get in the van and watch me pull out.

I'm on the highway for only a few minutes before I have to look in the rearview mirror because I want to prove to myself that what I'm feeling is not that monkey's eyes on me. But the monkey is looking into the mirror, too, right at me, right at my face, quiet, serious, not like it's accusing me or anything, just solemn, just serious. I flip the mirror up and drive the rest of the way without it.

Usually, when we score, we stash the goods at a locker, or at one of Scissors' cribs if the game is his, but there aren't any goods to stash, so I head home. The Town Car is hot, and I decide to lose it in a neighborhood where no one knows me, about a mile from my block. I remove the false plates and I lay them on top of the monkey's cage with the monkey inside it. It's maybe three in the morning by now, but if anyone is looking, they're making a mental note of me carrying a monkey in a cage with license plates.

I'm at my place turning the key in the lock, when I realize that even though we're not closed up inside the car anymore, and even though the cage has a live monkey in it, not a dead one, it really does reek. There's shit all over it, and I know I'm going to have to clean it and I'm worried about how to get the monkey clean—will I have to touch it, for instance?

I take the cage straight to the bathroom, and I do something I know I'll regret—I turn off my cell phone.

It's only a studio apartment, my place, just a box with a strip of kitchen on one side and a bathroom so narrow I can sit on the john and lean over to wash the monkey. Cleaning the monkey is not as disgusting as I thought it would be. I have to believe changing a human diaper is worse. It doesn't resist when I take it out of the cage and it hardly weighs anything, so I can hold it away from me and only my hands get dirty. In fact, it's so light I have this moment of panic that maybe it's not real—maybe I'm imagining the monkey, hallucinating. But I get a noseful of the stink, and that settles me.

The monkey is thin like a little kid. It doesn't make a sound and hardly moves the whole time I wash it. (I wonder, maybe the dead monkeys shocked all the sound out of it, maybe the horror took its voice.) I use my Dial soap, like I would on myself. I don't turn on the shower in case it would scare the monkey, so I have to work the soapy shit out of its fur with handfuls of water, which takes a long time. It doesn't squirm or act impatient. Once, though, its butt slips and its head goes back, and I reach for its arms at the same time it reaches for mine. Little dark hands grab my wrists, and I pull the monkey up from the water. The palms are rough, scratchy, but that's not what bothers me. It's when I look at them, at the thin dark fingers, my eyes fill up and I have to squeeze my face to keep from acting like a fool. I know the monkey is watching me, but I don't look back.

I had dogs I washed in the tub. With dogs, you rub them hard to dry them and they get loony and playful, but I'm pretty sure I shouldn't be rough with the monkey, so I pat it dry with my one ragged bath towel. Now that the shit's washed out of its coat, I can see it better. It isn't one of those space monkeys, chimpanzees, which are apes, not monkeys. It's smaller than that and has long, skinny arms, and a very long tail, and it's covered in reddish fur, also long, with lighter, shorter hairs around its eyes and mouth. I've seen kids like that, starved-looking, big eyes, crazy puffs of hair stuck up around their heads. And of course, I've seen some kids looked that serious.

When the monkey's not dripping anymore, I put it on the floor while I rinse the cage off. Then I sit the monkey in the cage on one end of the towel and drape the other end over its shoulders to keep it warm. It looks like a little Buddha, not the happy kind, one that's got the sorrow of the world on him. And even though it doesn't stink anymore, it's giving off this other thing, this cloud you can feel, not see, of sadness.

And then I can't think what I should do for the monkey. I can't concentrate because I'm back at the house listening. Listening for the Ford, the way the tires squeal taking the fork. Putting everything I've got into listening, like I expect the old man to catch us at something—like living, maybe. I'm in those seconds when we know the pickup is getting closer, that maybe he's got some food for us this time, but maybe he doesn't. That maybe we'll be too sick with fear to eat anyway. Every second pushing me to a choice—to run or not.

And I think food. When was the last time the monkey ate? Maybe all the monkey needs is food and its spirits will pick up. Something in me knows this is not true, but I have to resist the inevitable. I have to make it harder for Destiny to play me.

I try to think what I know monkeys eat, besides bananas. I don't have bananas. Other fruit, I think, and maybe bugs. I have plenty of bugs, but not handy, not corralled. I have some peaches, and grapes.

In the fridge, I find a peach that is still more peach than mold, so I cut off the good parts and pull off the best grapes and bring everything to the monkey, spread it around the monkey where it can reach. It doesn't move. I try the peaches and grapes, and then Rice Chex, and Ritz crackers (with peanut butter). I hold a cracker to the monkey's mouth and make Mmmm noises. I take a bite to show it. The monkey looks at me, and then it looks away. It's got this thing, this dignity, and it's killing me.

It's morning by now, and the city noises pick up—the birds and the traffic. Delivery vans, horns, the crackle of the broken sidewalk underfoot. People laughing, belching, swearing. My own building shaking itself awake. And then I hear the humping sound of bass in a ride passing by. And I think music. The walls are like paper in my building, but I figure it's late enough that music won't disturb the neighbors, which is important, not annoying the neighbors, when most of what you have you don't own.

So I turn on the stereo system I kept from a haul a couple of years ago. It's got decent sound, only the receiver gets a lot of static on the AM stations. I have a hot-jazz-and-low-down blues CD collection, but when I look at the monkey, I think "soothing" is what it needs, and since I hate easy-listening, I surf the FM stations until I find some classical stuff. No response from the monkey, but I leave it on. I get myself a beer and shift my armchair to where I can keep an eye on the monkey, checking it only once in a while, being real subtle, so I don't alarm it with my attention. Whenever the music changes, a voice ID's each track, the musicians and conductors and composers and other stuff. This goes on for a while, until I'm thinking of switching stations. Then the monkey moves.

The station has just put on this very pretty piece of music, sort of genteel and flowing and gut-wrenching at the same time, the way classical music can get, and the monkey stands up. It stands up and puts its hands on the bars of the cage. This makes me jump, and I stand up, too. The monkey's eyes are wider than they were before, and its mouth is open like it's about to say something, something wise, or something to make your heart split open. It grips the bars so hard I worry it's having some kind of fit, so I turn off the music. But this really upsets the monkey. It starts doing this thing with its hands— wringing them—that's what you would call it in a human, wringing its hands, only slowly, like a very, very old man, like someone senile, someone with Alzheimer's and all the time in the world to wring. So I turn the music back on, and it stops twisting its hands and puts them back on the bars. I open the cage and let the monkey out.

It doesn't tear out of there. It creeps, using its hands and its legs. It moves sideways towards the music, crabbing along the floor, its tail floating after it like it's held up with a wire, and it comes to a stop in front of one of the speakers. And it just sits there with its hands on its knees, still serious, still silent, listening. But the monkey is happy. I can tell because it's not giving off that sadness like it was before.

I'm trying not to believe that the monkey loves this piece of music, just this one. I am worried about what a thought like that would say about my sanity, but then, I am a guy who risked his life for a monkey. And even if it's true, I can't record off the radio, not with my equipment. Still, when the music ends and the voice tells us what we were listening to, I pay attention. Quartet for Strings in G K 80 Adagio by Mozart.

Another piece begins, and right away the monkey changes. It droops. It sags so that its little chin is on its chest. It moves in close and puts an arm around a speaker and slumps against it, limp, like it gives up. Like it's grieving for the music that is gone. And then it looks at me, and I know the look. I know I'm going to have to buy that quartet piece, get it on CD, and play it for the monkey all the time because what it's been through, it deserves the music it wants. And anyway, I know, without the music, the monkey will die.

There are obstacles. I can't leave the monkey to go shopping for the CD—it could die all alone—but I can't take a monkey in a store. I know from experience that the only CDs a fence will turn over these days are rap and hip-hop. You won't find Mozart on the street. And I can't order from home. For one thing, the CD might not get here in time, and anyway, I don't have a credit card—not in my name. I have plenty of credit cards in other names, but I only use them on the move and never have anything sent to my address. This never bothered me before. But now—the stolen cards, the lack of credit, the cash-flow situation—it's like I'm not just letting the monkey down now, at this moment, when we need that CD. I've been letting the monkey down my whole life.

So, I have to try. I use this phone book I scored from a public booth, and even though I don't know how I'll be able to pick up the CD, I make the calls. (When I turn on the cell, I see Nick's been trying to reach me. I ignore the messages and dial.) I call music stores. I call electronics stores. Even bookstores, the kind that sell more book-stuff than books. Some of these stores, they've got other Mozarts—other quartets in other letters and other numbers. But no Quartet for Strings in G K 80. So I keep trying. Musical instrument stores, gift stores, and all the stores that these stores send me to, like museum stores and stationery stores—any store anyone can think of.

When I run out of places to call, I turn off the cell again. Then I take point, sitting where I can see the monkey, the door and out the window, below to the street. It's still beautiful out, like the night before, and it stays that way, right into dusk, and even though you can't see the stars in the city, I think for minute about the clearing where we opened the trailer. The little frogs that stopped chirping when I passed.

Sometimes I took my sister with me, sometimes I didn't. It depended on what I heard in the way the old man ran the corners, in how he slammed the gears, how fast he was driving, how dangerous he was.

We hid in the woods by the marsh until he slept it off. Shared my sleeping bag under a rhododendron, shivering into the dawn. I took point, pinching myself to keep from drifting off. Sometimes he came looking for us, so hot his anger hit us like waves before he even got close, before we could smell the liquor fug that stuck to him. Before the frogs stopped chirping. When they did stop, my heart died, over and over, until they picked up again and we knew that he'd stumbled back to the house. Sometimes he was so bad, he pitched into the marsh, swearing and screaming at the sawgrass, and I held my sister's hand to keep her quiet. Sometimes he passed out between us and home, and in the morning we'd come on him sleeping like a dead man while we stole our way back.

When the door buzzer sounds, I jerk awake. I can't believe it. I'm point man and I nodded off standing point. That's a bullet in the back of the head on most teams, so it's no surprise I'm in a sweat, rushing to the monkey to put it back in the cage. But I don't even reach the speaker before my door blows in, never mind knocking.

"Where the fuck you been?" Mickey shouts, "What the fuck is going on, Pete? Nick's been calling you! All fucking day!" He looks at me and at the monkey hugging the speaker. Someone's playing piano on the radio like he's trying to cover all the keys at once.

"Sorry, Mick, battery died," I lie. It's a lame-ass excuse, and he knows it, but there are so many things we don't want to have to say to each other.

"We got a gig for later tonight," Mickey reports, chopping his words like they're punches. "B-and-E, house-call. For Scissors." He puts a hand over his eyes and takes a breath. "Oak and 23rd, 11:30, white Olds sedan." Then he looks at me. Pleads. "Christ, Pete, be there. Don't fuck up. I *liked* you, man." I note the past tense. He turns away and heads out the door, and his voice gets hard again: "I fucking *mean* it, fuckhead!"

I can't refuse because the fact that Scissors came in with an offer and Nick took him up on it so soon after the trailer disaster is for my benefit. I know they are worried about my state of mind. They have to see if I've lost it or not. They're considering cutting me loose. And I'm worried, too. Because I'm going to take the monkey along on the job.

I leave my place early and circle around the block where the Olds is parked so they don't see me with the monkey before I want them to. Mickey's not there—I have to believe the monkey and the speaker and the music were too much for him. Instead, Nick's driving—that means me and Bernie inside, with Nick in the car taking our backs. My gut twists.

"What the fuck!" Bernie shrieks when he turns to catch me slipping the cage onto the backseat.

I can see Nick's profile, and it's not encouraging. His eyes are give-me-strength closed, and I figure Mickey has been filling him in. "Why'd you bring the monkey, Pete?" he asks, his voice dead calm. I see the index finger he holds up to keep Bernie from starting in on me. He's like a patient parent, or a nurse with a mental case.

"Just figured," I answer, but the Olds is still idling— we are not moving.

"Figured what, you crazy asshole?" sputters Bernie. His face is almost purple and he's clawing his way around the passenger seat to get at me, but Nick holds him back until he quits struggling and flops into his seat.

"Pete, we can't take the monkey on the job," Nick says in that same even voice. "It's a liability. First, it slows us down. Two, it's noisy—"

"Not this monkey—" I start, but his eyebrows go up and he tilts his head, just like teachers when you interrupt them, so I wait for him to finish.

"It's unpredictable, let's say, okay, Pete? Un-pre-*dic*-table. Plus—and this is a big plus, Pete—Scissors sees this monkey in this car on this job and we'll be mopping your brains off this nice vinyl interior for a week."

"Like 'Pulp Fiction,' Pete!" screams Bernie, "Pulp-fucking-Fiction!"

There's no good way to explain myself, but I give Nick what I've got. "It's dying, Nick. I can't leave it alone. You saw what it was like in that trailer." There is a suck of air as they both remember the stench, the little cages and their cargo of carcasses. "If it's going to die, I don't want it to be alone."

"I don't fucking believe this!" Bernie is beside himself. "Get the fuck *out*, man!"

"Shut up, Bernie!" Nick orders. He looks at the monkey. "It's sick, huh?"

"Yeah." I don't explain about Mozart.

"You gotta keep it in the car, Pete. It's gotta be alone that long. There's a blanket behind you you can put over it so it thinks it's night or something. Then nobody sees the monkey when we drop off the score."

"What!" The air around us shimmies at the pitch of Bernie's voice. "Are you out of your fucking mind?"

"We don't have a choice, Bern," says Nick, and I'm straining to hear how he says it. "It's a three-man job."

"We'll get somebody else—"

"It's a three-man job that's going down *now*." And for the first time Nick gets that dangerous voice, the one you don't contradict because you know it doesn't matter who is right and who is wrong, we are doing it his way. He glances at the monkey again and at me. "At least it doesn't stink anymore."

It has to hit Bernie why this is, that the guy he's been on twenty-some jobs with, the point man, the one they trust for point, washed the monkey, and he is so shocked that he can't even scream. And I know Nick's thinking the same thing. I know that's why Nick's letting me bring the monkey on this sensitive lick. Because any guy who would wash a monkey is too far gone to reason with. And I wonder what he's got planned.

Then Bernie says, "It looks bad. Maybe it's hungry."

"Won't eat," I say.

"Come on," says Bernie, considering this. "You try bananas?"

"Tried everything."

The idea of the monkey not eating makes him quiet for a moment.

"I got a Mounds Bar," he offers, digging in a pocket. "Monkeys love coconut, don't they?"

"Shut the fuck up!" Nick hisses. "We got a job to do, and we're cutting it close." But he's turning the key, so I figure we settled the monkey issue for now, though he doesn't understand, or I hope he doesn't yet, that I'm not leaving the monkey in the car, and certainly not under a blanket. It will think it's dead.

We get to the target about midnight, cruise by once. It's an old neighborhood, small houses, mostly brick, lower middle-class, mix of attention and neglect. We know about the homeowner because one of Scissors' customers installs carpets for a living, and this cokehead is in serious debt to Scissors. So the junkie is putting in wall-to-wall and he overhears the owner canceling his paper for a week while he's on vacation. The place itself is nothing special on the outside. It needs a paint job, and

I'm starting to wonder why we expect to find anything besides the usual 26-inch TV and cheap CD changer.

We park the Olds in the alley and wait a few minutes to make sure everything's quiet, and then we get out. I pull the cage toward me on the back seat, climb out with it and ease the car door closed, when I realize Nick has turned around to watch me. He sees I'm holding the cage, which I was supposed to leave in back under a blanket, and he doesn't say a word about it. My blood goes cold, but I swing on ahead of Bernie with the monkey in the cage, listening for anything I don't like the sound of.

Our intel is No Alarm, and it's true, there's no lawn sign or window sticker. No dogs start up, either, so I'm beginning to let myself relax. And even though they filled me in on the way, I'm not prepared for what we find inside when I shine the beam around. Sound-studio in the den and incredible playback in the living room—that's the reason for the carpet. A job like this makes our palms tingle because you can turn over recording equipment faster than just about anything. Everybody is a rock star these days.

Then I notice that one entire wall of the living room, the whole 16x8, is CDs. I'm itching to get at look at them, but I know the chances are slim this guy's got what I want.

We can't flick a switch because, even with the blinds down, some neighbor could spot a crack of light and wonder who the hell's in here. So we work by flashlight, relying partly on Scissors' intel from the junkie, partly on instinct, unhooking what's mobile and saleable and probably doesn't need special software. Bernie's our electronics expert. He spots the good stuff and knows how to handle it. (That has to be why Nick keeps him, I think.) Like I expect, I have to keep calming him down.

He's so excited by the score.

To my surprise, it's turning out to be a very sweet deal. I had myself convinced it was just an excuse for Nick and Bernie to wet me. We are making real progress, stacking goods by the door and slipping out to load the Olds—or Bernie slips out, because I like to stick close to the monkey. Nick loads the stuff and watches for trouble.

We're down to scraps and Bernie's busy admiring these mother-size speakers we have to leave because they won't fit in the car. I decide to swing the beam around the room one more time. The guy's labeled his CD shelves—they're alphabetical. So I ease over to the M section, and my breath catches when I find a couple hundred Mozarts. I glance at Bernie, who's got his back to me. My heart is pumping so hard now, it's making me dizzy. I run a finger along the titles and pull out a 2-disk case with quartets. I know exactly what is going to happen, I know it. The first CD has the String Quartet in G K 80. Adagio and all.

"What the fuck are you doing?" I jump. Bernie is right behind me. He's breathing hard, and I know it's a matter of seconds before he starts screaming for Nick.

I put my finger to my lips, which is a pretty strange thing to do under the circumstances. In fact, it is so strange, or I look so insane, that Bernie just nods. "Where can I play this?" I ask. We've already liberated all the guy's CD changers. Bernie points to the computer on a desk in the breakfast nook. I'm over there in a second and slip in the CD. When I have trouble getting sound, Bernie pushes me out of the way and presses some keys and the tracks come up on the screen. I point to the one I want.

The music comes out of those giant speakers, the ones Bernie's been fiddling with, and even though we keep the volume low, the sound seems to be inside us, in our heads. It's beautiful. At first I'm not sure it's the right Mozart. But the monkey knows.

"Look," I tell Bernie, and I shine my beam on the cage.

"Holy shit!" Bernie yells, and I slap a hand on his mouth.

The monkey is sitting with its hands on its knees and its eyes closed. It's got its head up, and its little body is sort of rocking back and forth to the music.

"It likes music, huh?" whispers Bernie.

"Not just any music," I say, and though it's stupid, I'm proud of the monkey for this. I'm bragging. "This music. This one piece of music. By Mozart."

"Not just any Mozart, huh?" says Bernie.

"This one piece."

We're quiet a minute. Then Bernie jumps up and runs into the kitchen. I hear the fridge open and see the dull glow from the door. It shuts and he's back with a couple of plastic bowls and an apple, and a dishtowel he wears on his arm like a waiter.

"We gotta get something down it while it's happy like this," he says.

We go to the cage, but I put a hand on his arm to stop him. "What've you got?"

"Looks like cream corn. And peas-and-carrots."

I think for a minute. "Try the corn."

The room light snaps on and we freeze. It's Nick, but I almost wish it was the police. He's got his piece out pointed at us. Bernie doesn't get it right away and starts screaming, "Hey! Turn out the fucking light! We'll have every fucking cop in the—" And Nick shoots him. In the chest. The sound is so loud in my ears that I think, That ought to bring someone here before it's my turn. But that's just wishful thinking.

Bernie falls against the living room couch, the bowls flying out of his hands, and he is gurgling, trying, probably, to scream. The brand-new carpet is splashed with creamed corn, not to mention blood. Peas and carrots are scattered over everything like confetti. He's dead before Nick reaches him. Even though he's wearing gloves, Nick wipes his gun hard with the towel Bernie brought from the kitchen and shifts it to his left hand. Then he reaches inside Bernie's jacket, pulls out Bernie's piece and points it at me.

"A fucking monkey, Pete. What were you thinking?" He looks like he wants to cry. I know the plan—shoot me with Bernie's gun, wipe it clean and stick it in Bernie's dead hand, just like he wiped the other, which goes in mine. Scissors will cut him some slack about the bad lick because Nick had to take care of this other problem.

But Nick doesn't shoot me, not yet. He turns to the cage. "A fucking monkey," and I know what he's going to do, so I dive for the light switch and hit it just in time. "Shit!" says Nick as the gun goes off, and I hope to hell he missed the monkey.

I know he'll have to lose one gun to reach into his pocket for his flashlight, and in that time I go for him, knocking him down so hard I shake the other gun out of his hand. We roll around in the dark grunting and slugging. He tries pressing on my carotid to make me pass out, but I jam him up under the jaw with my flashlight. And then I'm just smashing at him in the dark, smashing and smashing until there's no sound except the wet kind that makes your gut jolt.

When I'm sure he's not moving, I stumble to the light switch and flip it. I have to squint in the light, and at first I think the monkey's been hit. It's a ball of fur on the bottom of the cage. But then I see the hands moving, twisting over and over, and I realize the music's changed. In the distance I hear a siren. I go to the computer and start the Adagio again the way I saw Bernie do it, and the monkey sits up, so I get a good look at it. It doesn't seem to be hurt anywhere.

Bernie's eyes are open. A bloody foam spills from his mouth down his chin. Nick is a pulpy mess on the floor beside him. I'm wet, and when I look down at myself, there's blood soaked into my clothes from my shoulders to my crotch. It's not mine—it's Nick's.

But the monkey is happy. I can tell.

From the sound of the siren, I figure we've got one, maybe two minutes. I can let the monkey listen to the Mozart a minute or two longer.

The monkey is swaying to the music, and in another minute I'll lift it out of the cage and put it on my shoulder. I'll put the CD in my pocket and we'll leave together in the Olds. I've got two guns and both flashlights, both flashlights and both of them work. Two Lorcins, eighteen rounds left. There's a place I know in the marshes where we'll make our stand. Past a wall of sawgrass and a moat of swamp. A safe place, where we'll listen all day and all night to Mozart's String Quartet in G K 80 Adagio. And there, in the dark, all around us, a thousand little frogs will chirp, a thousand little frogs standing point.

DETAILS

On the eve of his fifty-fifth birthday, Evan Rhys began drinking coffee at night. Not decaf. Real coffee. One cup, and late, not long before bed. He introduced the idea to his wife Helen as they stood side-by-side at the kitchen counter, she rinsing plates and flatware and glasses, he loading the dishwasher. She stopped what she was doing and looked at him, puzzled but smiling.

"Won't it keep you awake? Doesn't the doctor want you to cut down on *caffeine*?"

Even though he expected this gentle interrogation, Evan winced at the word "doctor," which, like "checkup" and "blood work" and "prostate," and, especially, "colonoscopy," had taken on a suggestion of decay since he had received his introductory issue of the AARP bulletin five years earlier. ("But I'm not a 'Retired Person,' " he had protested at the time, his voice breaking with distress, like a teenager's.)

Now he cooed reassuringly, "I know. But I have a taste for coffee right this moment, and it will help me stay up to finish my reading." Helen cocked her head, giving him her fondly indulgent look. "Tell you what," he suggested, "I'll skip my morning latte tomorrow. That should more than make up for it."

To hide his dismay over "doctor," he bent over the rack of porcelain platters she had thrown on her wheel and painted and fired and glazed for him twenty years earlier. These were patterned in a wildly imaginative swirl of dark-hued blues, with bright spots of other colors here and there, and amorphous forms. ("They're planets, Daddy, see?" his children had always insisted. "And the little whitish ones are stars.") Planets and stars. And Earth, of course: they picked it out every time, amused that no matter how he held the plate to the light, he was never able to identify their world. He always took special care to stack the dishware safely, but several pieces had chipped over time. Now he absently picked at a crack, worrying it. (*Doctor*) He straightened up and looked at his wife. Still watching him and smiling, Helen shook her head slightly, and the silver Indian pendant earrings he had given her because he could not wait to delight her jingled softly. He stroked her arm.

It was not Evan's birthday that had triggered the uncharacteristic impulse to make himself a mug of coffee at such an hour. It was Helen's. Earlier that morning, Helen, who was to turn fifty in ten days, had received her own first mailing from the AARP. He gave her the earrings right then to soften the blow. But while Evan had immediately disposed of his bulletin with its ominous membership subscription enclosure, she read hers, front to back, deliberately and with the kind of interest that made her lips open loosely. As he watched her covertly over the student paper he was grading, it occurred to Evan for the first time that his wife was getting old.

"Oh, Helen, there can't be anything interesting in it, can there?"

She giggled and shot him a sly glance.

That night, he began drinking real coffee before bedtime. Evan had a deliberateness about him, so people thought him methodical by temperament, but that wasn't really the case. It was just that he knew himself well; he was too easily distracted—by a lilting glance of light, by some kinds of laughter, by a child's sigh, by the beauty of his wife. He had to plan carefully, in detail, to get anything done. So now, after he rinsed his coffee mug (Helen again: feathered clay with a shimmery glaze that made it look lighter than it was), and once he returned to his Morris chair and to the stack of journals which never seemed to decrease in size, he checked his watch before opening to the last article he meant to read that night.

Fifteen minutes into it, he lifted his eyes from his reading to share an idea that he thought would interest Helen. This night, it was a paragraph on Ruskin (the famous figured carpet and Turner's canvases). But in the future, it might be anything, a quotation, a picture, an idea that he thought would amuse her. The important thing was that he timed this moment, allowing just thirty seconds to make his observation and elicit and acknowledge her response. Then he read for another ten minutes and, finally, he asked, "Time for bed?"

Helen looked up from the bulletin (he could just make out a headline: "Real Men See Doctors") and smiled. "Yes, I am tired. Let's go up, Evan."

They climbed the stairs, each with an arm hooked around the other's waist, and at first he thought that it was this intimacy that was responsible for the small tremor of guilt that shot through him. But then it was gone, and after all, it could have been his heart quickening with the coffee (caf-*feine* caf-*feine* caf-*feine*). He had left just this amount of time (fifteen minutes of reading, thirty seconds of talk, ten more minutes of reading) for the Colombian dark roast to kick in, really kick in, so that he would be able to outlast her.

That first night, with two hours to go until he would turn fifty-five, after he had shared his thoughts about the critic and the painter and Helen had laughingly quoted from her first AARP bulletin ("It says here that twenty-five percent of women over sixty have sex once a week"), after they had mounted the stairs, dealt with their teeth, pulled back the sheets and climbed in, he only had to wait a few minutes before her steady breathing told him he could make his move.

He knew exactly what he was looking for. It was his favorite place on her, that curve, that dip in the waist and rise to the hip, like a cello's, the one really beautiful—as opposed to coarse—thing that made a woman different from a man. It was like poetry every time he encountered it, her hip. It was like a swell in music, a roll of waves. It was the first thing he was afraid of losing to age, to decay, and this night he felt compelled to check on its condition, to gauge his loss, to bid it good-bye.

Evan prided himself on being a detail man, and this was the kind of inspection he couldn't have managed during sex. He would need his glasses—otherwise, he would be forced to practically press his nose against her for a good look. Not surprisingly, intimacy made them fog, and they could get tangled in Helen's hair or crushed beneath their two bodies.

So he needed her inert, unconscious, while, hopped up on joe, he would have all the time in the world to find the evidence and indulge his dismay. And he had secured this time, had succeeded thus far with his careful planning. But this first night, he hadn't been able to think beyond the bed and her sleeping form, and of course, his wakefulness. Now, new obstacles presented themselves. For one thing, although she was positioned as usual on her side and turned from him, the hip was under the covers. He didn't know how to get past them without waking her, and if she did catch him, he'd have to explain the glasses. But the glasses were made irrelevant by another, and worse, difficulty. It was dark, of course. So instead of making his move that first night, he worked out the rest of his plan. He had a booklight, the kind you strapped to your head like a miner's lamp. He would pretend to be reading when she fell asleep; that would explain the light—and the glasses—if she woke to find him so equipped.

Helen was always a heavy sleeper. Still, the next night, after coffee, after reading, after his comment ("another article on nineteenth-century narrative painting and the rise of the mystery novel") and her response ("Did you know that P. D. James is 84?"), after ten more minutes of reading ("Let's go up" ... "Yes, let's"), after she had taken him in her mouth ("Happy birthday, darling"), after he had adjusted his headlamp and glasses, after he felt the weight of her relax next to him and knew she slept . . . still, still, he was nervous. His palms sweated and his hands shook and his heart hit his ribs (caf-*feine* caf-*feine*) as he burrowed under the covers and trained the light on that spot. He had intended to check first for some thickening of the waist, to see if he could detect some change. Was that dip not quite as deep as he remembered, the cant not so canted? Was it now a beginner's slope, so to speak, as opposed to the Giant Slalom? Then he was interested in its texture, as well. Crepeyness. He would check for that consistency like crushed fabric that heralded the demise of cells. But a curious thing happened once he began his examination. He found he was distracted by the familiar contour of her, the odor of her and their lovemaking, and suddenly he was transported to his first encounter with this hip.

He was in graduate school in 1973, a diligent research assistant and a competent TA, but a callow lover. His stick-figure physique, pale skin and already thinning hair had attracted few opportunities to sharpen his sexual skills. There had been two co-eds in college, one broodingly Pre-Raphaelite, a Jane Morris beauty, but bulimic and self-conscious and unwilling to have sex in the nude ("I hate my body!"). The other, hard muscled, fiercely predatory and bisexual, was attracted to him because of his very ineptitude, which she seemed to find endearingly effeminate ("You sweet thing!"). Neither of these young women had encouraged the kind of foreplay in which he so desperately needed practice. More recently, there had been the department secretary, pinched and angular and, he rejoiced to discover, experienced. But she was impatient, as well, and had become so contemptuous of him that it made him nervous to think of his curriculum vitae passing through her hands on the way to hiring committees.

Then he saw Helen at an art exhibit arranged by his dissertation director. It was poorly attended; he couldn't even get his few friends to go ("Victorian art? An oxymoron!"). The exhibit was heavily hung with lengthy analyses of the paintings (his mentor's contribution) in terms of the Iconography of Industrialization: railroads, factories and mines figured in gloomy prominence.

"Not a Rosetti or a Millais among them!" she said, cheerfully returning his gaze. Snow-white skin, hair black as ebony, ruby-red lips—he had stumbled into a fairy tale.

"A little color would have done them some good, don't you think so? A little *en plein air*, painting on white-washed canvas. Something luminous." She could have been describing herself, the lushness of her made such a contrast to the mills and smokestacks.

"And detail," he added lamely. "I mean like Millais, or-or Hunt—detail—I mean—"

"Yes, yes," she laughed. "I know what you mean. It needs that. Nothing invites inspection, does it?"

He listened to her boisterous critique, and really didn't listen. Didn't really listen to Helen, of all people—she who, he would come to learn, could turn clay pots so that they appeared to be made of fine threads of spun sugar. He didn't listen because that dirge of an exhibit suddenly became irrelevant as love sucked the wind out of him all in a blow.

It would be incorrect to describe Helen as fat, but it was characteristic of women to starve themselves into oblivion then as now, and she stood out. Content to be a size twelve in a world of fours and sixes, she had full hips, defined by a real waist. The hips of Millais' Mariana, he liked to think.

They went to bed together on the night of that first day. That day, when he had fallen so hard in love with her that he had forgotten to eat, to comb his hair, to meet with his dissertation director or hand in his research results to the professor who employed him. A day when he couldn't not be with her, so that he haunted the hallways during her classes and held his bladder lest she slip away from him while he was urinating. It was on that night, when she moved his hands for him, brought his face to hers and to her body. It was the moment he saw and felt that curve. It was then that he knew what to do—everything, what to touch, what to lick, how long and when. He moved with a grace and a confidence with which he surprised and delighted himself. He brought her to climax again and again. And when it was over, he rested a long time with his head cradled there, in the crook of waist, his lips against her hip.

He had precedents for his fetish, as he guessed it would be called. Man Ray's photograph *"Le Violon d'Ingres,"* several poets, and many, many painters whom Helen, though unaware of his obsession, had introduced to him since then. Nevertheless, he wondered why he was convinced that this precious spot would be the first to go. Maybe it was the cartoon image in his mind of middle-aged women: one straight line from their armpits to their thighs, the only evidence of *la différence* being the big bosoms that rested contently on their stomachs. Women who looked like men dressing like women. Even the starved ones, the ones who wore suits pinched at the waist to maintain the illusion of a figure, were at best weight-trained and tread-milled to the consistency of beef jerky. Apparently, middle-aged women either had no hips or were all hip.

Now, on the night of his fifty-fifth birthday, as he crouched under the covers, with the booklight trained on her, Helen became his *madeleine*, and he let his chance slip, all of his senses coalescing into an attitude of profound worship.

He couldn't focus, couldn't concentrate his anxiety on that spot. It made him giddy, and . . . finally, he gave it up, carefully kissing the dint of flesh and turning away from her, still accoutered in his headlamp and glasses, content to savor the aftertaste of his own personal *temps perdu* for several wakeful hours until the Colombian dark roast finally released him.

And so Evan entered into a routine, both to train himself for his midnight reconnaissances and to escape his wife's suspicion by making this ritual an accepted regularity. He drank his nightly cup of coffee, timed his reading and conversation, coaxed Helen to bed, donned his headlamp and . . . read, usually. But once in a while, he would attempt another visit to that buckle of flesh, always to experience again such a vertiginous ecstasy of remembered bliss that he never really knew if it was the hip that was intact, or only his memory of it. Sometimes, she threw him another kind of curve, as she had on his fifty-fifth birthday, rubbing her leg against the back of his thigh and reaching around from behind him to stroke his chest, his midriff, making his jumped-up heart lurch dangerously and then continue to pound (caf-*feine* caf-*feine* caf-*feine*) all during their lovemaking. But the silver lining to this interruption in his plans was that she slept deeply after sex, wholly unconscious to anything he might say or do. He could even move her without her waking.

Both of their birthdays had come and gone, and having maintained the nightly coffee habit as his cover, he decided to undertake a new examination, this time of another cherished spot. It was the hollow in the back of her knee, the repository of many kisses, trove of treasures, cup of concupiscence. Peeping out beneath the hem of her skirt, it could send an oddly tender frisson through him at cocktail parties. He was anxious to know if it had been invaded by tiny tracks of veins, rising through the softening tissue, rendering her flesh a map of sanguinary rivulets.

There was no lovemaking this night. They had eaten dinner at Pino's Pizza and Pasta, or "P-Cubed," as the students called it, and it sat heavily on Helen. (He had been careful to leave the table still hungry.) She fell asleep almost the moment she turned from him. He could smell the garlic on her skin, and it occurred to him, as it had frequently in the past, that women should always smell like food, not like those cloying confections of expensive scents meant to attract men. He particularly loved her to smell like butter, and, for some reason, cloves. Now as he approached the spot (shadow of pent promises) and maneuvered himself so that the light would expose it in a way that a bedside lamp never could, he felt the same dizzying rush he had when encountering her hip, the sense that time had somehow collapsed, or more accurately, melted, and he enjoyed again the flush of youthfulness and the restored impact of his first engagement with this miniature vortex. And so, as he had when he put his lips to her hip, he was forced to come away from his researches with no clear image of the current state of the spot, that tiny chasm. But again, the relived moment—commingled with the scent of garlic— lingered, this time sustaining him even through the next few days (particularly when he found himself in the neighborhood of Italian cooking).

"You have a bounce in your step, these days, Evan," Mansard, his colleague and co-director of the Victorian Studies program, announced to him with barely suppressed envy. "Not indulging in monkey glands, are we?" The antiquarian's equivalent of a Viagra joke, formerly this would have irritated Evan, but now he smiled the same secret smile that had glowed back at him from bus windows and washroom mirrors when as a young man he had floated through the early months of passion with Helen. He would say that his expeditions to those fleshly shrines had made him a new man, but in fact, they had made him a *renewed* man, his old young self again.

When they first met, Helen had the kind of heavy long black tresses that collected smells—of food, of course, and cigarettes, which in those days acted as an aphrodisiac rather than the reverse—but also of her musk, and wood fires, and potter's clay. It had stabbed him to the heart when he lifted her hair for the first time to kiss the back of her neck, the nape, where it touched her shoulders. The dark of that heavy wealth ended with such conviction there against her sun-starved skin. When they were students, he would wait for her in the university's art museum, where she had an internship, and venturing into the Far East collection one day, he was struck immobile by encountering that very place on the neck of a beauty in an Utamaro print. This geisha gazed wistfully at her mirror with her back to the viewer. A small, fine hand rested in the crook of her neck, guiding the viewer's eye to the focal point of the picture, the nape. There, the hair made two dark points down the back of her white neck. The points and the fingers of the slender hand met at that spot which on his wife could dissolve his heart and loins. From that moment he collected "*bijinga*," *ukiyo-e* of beautiful women, but only those which offered a rear perspective and exposed the neck.

Helen's hair had pewtered over the years; she kept it long, though, and the contrast with her still-dark brows could overwhelm him with its drama. But she rarely wore her hair up, and certainly not in bed, so it was a special challenge to examine the condition of the nape of her neck. Of course, one advantage was that he could carry on his inspection in the open, above the comforter. He chose a night when her hair was not caught in the fold of linens at her shoulders, but mostly lay spread in vinous ropes across her pillow. Still, enough obscured the nape that he knew he would have to find a way to move it. His hand trembled as he gently pulled the tresses from the collar of her silk nightshirt and brought his face to her neck. She shifted slightly and one hand came up to rest, like the geisha's, in the crook of her neck, sending him into the now familiar erotic tailspin. He released her hair and, as he had with hip and knee, resigned himself to savoring the sensations the nape had aroused.

He did, from time to time, wonder how Helen could sleep through the tumult she caused in his heart. If his crawling around beneath the blanket didn't waken her, or the frequent "chink-chink" of his headlamp as it slipped down against the frames of his glasses, surely the electricity generated from his overtaxed heart and heated imagination would. But, though she sometimes sighed and shifted in her sleep, sometimes muttered, sometimes snored, she never opened her eyes, never turned an alarmed face on him; her black brows never knit themselves in dismay. Not once was he forced to explain the odd picture he must make.

He thought she might be feigning sleep. But she never raised the subject in the daylight, carrying herself, as always, with the calm joy, the complacence with her life, that allowed her to let her hair gray, to eat what she liked, to turn out a prodigious number of excellent pottery bowls and mugs and vases which never sold, to receive the AARP bulletins and magazines and special offers as though they did not constitute a sentence of death.

Nothing he did to her at night ever registered in her morning smile.

Meanwhile, in public, Evan could feel himself shine with an inner warmth; he positively glowed at faculty gatherings. When Helen accompanied him, it took only the suggestion of that hip beneath the cotton tunic she wore over her skirt, only a peek at her knee that whispered what secret place it hid, for him to shake off the crust of age and move among his colleagues with new luster. And when she was not with him, just the anticipation of meeting his young wife again with his young self buoyed his spirits during the most soul-deadening papers or tedious luncheon lectures and even lent him a sort of attraction. Beth Watkinson put her foot on his under the table at the Midwinter Forum, and he simply smiled at her and checked his watch. Dick Seidersmith asked him to make a fourth at tennis.

Evan's students suddenly found him interesting for the first time in several years and hung on his every word, as on a guru's. He brought them home, where they met Helen, and, because they were young and their radar for such things was very sensitive, they picked up on the chemistry between this man and wife, who "weren't old, really, not as old as most of the faculty. And you could tell they still loved each other, still had sex." These young people in his home, flushed with wine and admiration, stimulated him, so he waxed eloquent and joked freely, and when he had seen them out, he even opted for some real sex and sleep, instead of coffee and memories.

As the sacred places on his wife's body came to elevate Evan through his days, his nighttime pilgrimages to them became less frequent. Finally, some months after his first exploration, he stopped suddenly while loading the dishwasher and gazed stupidly at the platter in his hands.

"Oh, look, it's the earth," he said, and then blushed.

Helen laughed. "You and the kids."

"I never saw it before now."

"Of course you did."

He saw the earth that night, and its place in the yawning universe, saw its continents, some of them, and its seas. He felt himself skimming along the stratosphere, the familiar comforting lights blinking at him from below, the dark and peaceful patches of sea between them.

"Don't you want your coffee?" his wife remarked as he settled in for a comfortable read.

"Oh, not tonight. I'm a little acidic, I think." He smiled at her. "Nothing serious." And Helen smiled back.

That night Evan Rhys gave up coffee. Entirely. Even decaf with its trace caffeine. After all, he reasoned, there was a great deal now to live for. The woman of his dreams was still there. She was all there.

WINGS

Maeve held onto her condo until the "heart episode," as the doctor called it. Then her grandson Brian and his wife stepped in and insisted she move in with his family. They'd a large house and two salaries and wouldn't hear of her giving them money, but settled her in the first-floor "in-law suite," and shopped for her special foods and medicines, and ferried her to and from the doctor and elsewhere. They couldn't know what it meant to her, not to be put in a nursing home, or worse still, sent back to Ireland.

She hadn't said so to Brian, but living alone in her own place had become dismaying: it allowed too much time for memories, the kind that pushed their way into the very room you were sitting in and sat alongside you like a presence, until you started imagining things were what they weren't. Until the soot of them left you with black thoughts. You woke up with the burden heavy upon you, the dark mist in your eyes, forgetting where you were and wondering at the four walls of the bedroom. You caught a glimpse in the mirror made your heart leap to your throat—and then you recognized yourself. A body's own company was no more than cold comfort.

Maeve's dicky heart and her gammy legs meant there wasn't much she could do to repay Brian and Shelly, save to mind their two little girls in the afternoons. And she managed some light—very light—housework, but it hardly seemed enough. So she promised her great-granddaughters homemade Hallowe'en costumes, whatever they chose to be. Her hands were a horror to look at, her fingers bulging and curling like the roots of ancient trees, but even at eighty-four, she could still work a needle with fair skill. And she was that grateful to be there that she made the offer without thinking.

"A faerie, Grammy O'Neal!" the older girl Erin piped up, and Maeve's hand flew to her mouth in horror.

She should have known better than to leave it to two little girls, but she was careless from living so long in America, where it isn't the same as open promises made in Ireland that brought curses down upon you and your descendants. Here they spelled and said it "fairy," leaving out the dangerous part, the evil part, that keening in the middle of the word. They'd no notion of real faeries—Disney took care of that—the kind left behind in Ireland, the kind that kept close in the last forsaken places and nurtured their grievances against mankind, turning bitterness and glee over and over like marbled dough as they made their plans. Here, stories of the kind Maeve could tell would be put down to fancy, or madness.

"I want to be a faerie!" persisted Erin.

And of course, her little sergeant Bridey had to have the same as well. "Me, too, G'ammy 'Neal, a faerie, a faerie!"

The moment the word was spoken, Maeve caught a whiff of sulfur in the air and a whinny of triumph. But it was just the garbage collector's truck in the alley behind them, the smell of rot and the sound of the brakes. Not a pooka, she scolded herself, it was the dustman was all.

She pulled herself together. She gave them a smile. "Oh, wouldn't you rather be princesses, then, loveys? I'll sew you beautiful elegant gowns, and we'll make crowns with veils of lace."

But their faces fell. And later at dinner they blabbed to their father and mother about the faerie costumes, so that Maeve could see she was expected to sew them.

"Well, but there is only one Tinkerbell," she tried to discourage them a last time, "and you can't both be that." This did make the littler one, Bridey, furrow her brow a bit, but Erin was too quick for it.

"I'll be some other faerie," she reassured her sister. "A made-up one." And just like that it was settled.

It was impossible to sleep that night, thinking about it. Back in County Sligo, she hadn't known a single neighbor hadn't lost something precious to them. They were wicked evil, the faeries back home. Fortunate those who just lost their goods or livestock, less fortunate the ones who lost a man or wife or child, the worst the ones who lost their souls, of course. Maeve had known them, too. You had to be careful what you wished for and what you cherished. The boasting of your luck, for instance, brought the headless dullahan to you, a terrible thing. And anyone knew not to make too much of a child. That was one way to bring their envy upon you, the fussing over a child. They'd take the dear one and leave one of their own vile brood in its place. The O'Hallorans' girl was proof. When Maeve's own Caoilin was born back in Ireland, she remembered little Sinéad O'Halloran's dead eyes, and she was careful to love her own baby solemnly and dress her crib with iron tongs and drape it with her husband Frank's shirts, and it must have worked because she'd kept her darling girl with her for fifty-two years.

This is America, Maeve reminded herself. America might have its own kind of troubles with gangs and terrorists, but it was free of faeries, thank the Holy Mother. But she tossed and groaned, nonetheless, thinking that it was an invitation, a bold invitation, a challenge even, to the darkness. Finally, she got up to turn her slippers so that the toes pointed outward from her bed, placing one of her knee-high hose beneath the frame as well, for good measure. It harmed no one to indulge in a few old precautions.

They made an outing of buying the cloth and notions, herself and Shelly and Erin and the little one. There were bright days in the suburbs in America, even in the dying season, that made you forget the deep hollows back in Sligo, or the blackthorn trees, bristling with the lunantishee, who like nothing better than to sink their needle teeth into your flesh, unless it was they could catch a leprechaun, like a treat for them. Give her the jewel that was a crisp fall day in a Midwest shopping mall, where colorful goods smiled at you from many windows, and if there ever had been sprites that haunted the prairie, they'd been nudged to extinction by glass and concrete.

She could have spent all day in the fabrics shop, they'd such glorious stuff. Betsy Ross Fabrics, they'd named it, so she'd been afraid everything would be red, white and blue. But she was wrong as could be. To feel the stuff between her fingers was a pleasure worth the pain in her poor shanks and ankles. The girls were giddier than she'd ever seen them except at Christmas. That day of shopping was like Hallowe'en itself, or a circus or a play, with the East Indian women who worked at the counters and those who were buying silks for saris. They had shining trim on the hems of their scarves, and gold studs in their noses, and glistening skin, and it made her dizzy with the beauty of it all.

"What's wrong, Grammy?" asked Erin when Maeve put a hand on a bolt of blue satin to steady herself.

"'S'rong, G'ammy?" echoed Bridey, taking Maeve's free hand and patting it.

Shelly found her a chair—one of those molded plastic things, too small for Maeve's backside, but it was a relief to take the weight off. And from there she could watch the girls dance from table to table, while Shelley picked out bolts and swatches to ask her opinion.

"I'll have to leave it to you, Maeve," Shelly said, glancing at her watch. "I don't know what's easy to work with, what goes with what."

Maeve pushed out of her mind that they were after faerie costumes, whispering *princess* to herself. In the end, she chose the blue satin for Erin, the pink organza for the baby, with white tulle for a ruffled waist each. The pieces were cut and folded in a glistening pile, and the threads and other things collected.

"And wings?" asked Shelly, examining the mound of goods. "How do you make the wings?"

"Tired," mumbled Maeve. "I'm so tired, Shelly darling. Could we come back for the wings another time?"

Maeve was eight years old when she was witness to the O'Hallorans' misery, something she confessed to no one, not even her Grammy. They were on their way home after Mass one Sunday, Maeve's Grammy, the two mothers Eimhear O'Halloran and Maeve's own Ma, and the children—that was Maeve and her three brothers. And the changeling Sinéad.

"Could you give us a couple of fists of grain, Siobhan?"

Eimhear O'Halloran asked Maeve's mother. "I've just enough for a loaf, but I like it to thicken the stew." The two neighbor families were always sharing and giving to the other when they could.

"I can that, Eimhear," said Maeve's mother, hooking her arm into her friend's. Eimhear held onto Sinéad with her other hand, the changeling walking along in a trance, as usual. "Maeve'll carry it to you before tea."

No one even thought of sending Sinéad for the flour, though the thing was five years old, old enough to help a great deal around the parents' farm, and they had no other children. The dummy was useless. Its mind, if it had one, was always in the banquet halls or ballrooms of its faerie kin—or more probably, the filthy sties where they nested—so that it was never truly with you. The vacant place behind its eyes made your blood run cold.

Maeve ran as fast as she could to the farm, over the rocky rises, the grain wound tightly in her apron. Eimhear O'Halloran was to give her a small brick of lard wrapped in newspaper to take home with her the same way. It was early yet, not past two o'clock, but Maeve ran, for it was a dark day with the sky covered in black-petticoated clouds. She wasn't the only one didn't like to be out alone. Her brothers hated to cross the fields on their own, even though there were few enough trees and no deep dells between the two properties to hide any evil thing, even the tiny gancanagh, who seemed most innocent, tempting passersby with their leaping lights. But her Grammy had taught her no faerie was harmless: "Wherever you are, if you find yourself alone, you'll do well to keep your eyes to the ground before you and say a prayer loudly on your way."

So Maeve was reciting the Our Father when she heard the screaming, and her first thought was now she'd heard the banshee, and someone in her family would be dead by morning. But the screaming grew louder as she approached the glow that was the farmhouse kitchen window. By the time she reached the building, the scream had become a hooting moan, and, peering fearfully over the window ledge, she could see this was coming from Eimhear O'Halloran.

Maeve had never witnessed anything like Eimhear O'Halloran at that moment. It wasn't just her wild mane of hair, with its one dull streak of grey that marked her from the birthing of Sinéad, but that her face was all twisted and red and her teeth were bared. She held her hands as though she had claws to reach out and tear the flesh from anyone before her. And there *was* someone with Eimhear: it was her husband Cillian, and blood was oozing from deep scratches in his face.

Maeve thought right away that Cillian must be drunk. Her own Da got that way from time to time, which made her Ma weep and her Grammy say brittle things. Sometimes he got home so bad with the drink that he couldn't make it around back to relieve himself, so he watered the side of the house. "Just like a dog!" her Grammy would spit at him, while her mother put her head in her apron. Like her Da, Cillian must have come inside with his flies still undone, for he was struggling to button his trousers at the same time that he had to keep Eimhear from his face.

"You've ruined her, Cillian O'Halloran, ruined her!" shrieked Eimhear, now tearing at her hair. Just then, in the doorway appeared the pale changeling Sinéad, standing stiffly with its arms hard against its sides and with its shift rucked up to its waist so that the private place was showing. Its eyes were very wide. Maeve had never heard the thing Sinéad speak, but now it opened its mouth like a great fish and shrieked so loudly, so much more loudly than Eimhear had done, that Maeve had to put her hands to her ears.

Something was wrong with a house that had a changeling, and the scene before Maeve, while she wasn't to make sense of it until the next day, made her sick and desperate at the same time, so that she dropped her apron, forgetting about the grain, and ran home before anyone in that mad house noticed her. She didn't think she could talk about what she'd seen, and once she was standing outside the door to her own home, she fretted how to explain the lost wheat flour. But her mother had forgotten to expect the lard from Eimhear and never even asked about the errand at all. And the next evening, her Grammy came home from visiting an old friend in the village with news that made Maeve and her family think of nothing else.

"They're sending the thing to the children's asylum first light, and it's about time they faced what they had in their home!" Grammy said as she pulled at a crust with her few good teeth. Maeve's parents looked at each other, but were silent.

"Why are they sending her *now*, Grammy, when she's always been a dummy?" asked Maeve's brother Niall.

Grammy winked at him. "Well, that Cillian's gone too far, petting the child when she was still human and petting and petting the thing even now it's not. Touching its skin . . . and you know, after a while some of them, they can't abide the touch of a decent man. He brought it to scream last night, and it's not yet stopped to draw breath." She gave a stiff nod and worked the gluey bread into her cheek the better to be clearly heard. "Well, even those two that have lied to themselves have to admit, it's nothing human sounds like that. I'm sorry for them, they've only the one, but its better this way. It's not a real child, and they'll send it away to where it won't be thought so strange."

"I'll dip that crust for you, Mother; it's too hard on your gums," said Maeve's Ma the moment the old woman took a breath. "Give it here, Mother . . ."

But Grammy made a face and shook her head. She hated an interruption lest she lost her thread. As she spoke, she pointed at each of them to make them pay heed: "It was Eimhear put a stop to it. She took that man of hers in hand at last." When Ma and Da traded glances again, Grammy added, "I tell you, he's the reason they lost the child out of her crib in the first place!"

After that, though there were still chores undone, their Ma made them go to bed, and the grown people whispered together into the night. And Grammy that was Maeve's mother's mother, must have got into it once again with Maeve's Da—they were always pulling at some bone or other between them—for Maeve heard her father burst out, "Silly priest-ridden superstitious old cow!" before Maeve's mother could shush him.

Maeve spent every minute her fingers could bear on the girls' costumes. But even keeping herself busy like this, she lost herself more and more to dreadful thoughts, to the past, so that she fell into those practices her Grammy had taught her against magic folk, carrying protection in her pockets (an iron door hinge, a handful of oatmeal or acorns), putting pennies in the children's shoes, plucking scarlet threads from the sun-room throw pillows to work into a talisman. She had to stop herself with the family present, even when odd shadows appeared from nowhere or she picked up a hiss of whispers that skittered away as she strained to hear it. And she hid the evidence, turning the plucked cushions damage-side-down, emptying her pockets in the privacy of her toilet before dropping a soiled housecoat in the laundry basket.

Two days before Hallowe'en, Erin came home from kindergarten with a picture she'd drawn of her costume. Maeve right away noticed it had wings. Later, when she came to the kitchen to offer to help Shelly with dinner, Maeve spotted Erin's picture on the refrigerator.

"How are the costumes coming?" asked Shelly, her back to Maeve as she chopped vegetables.

"They're finished, I think," said Maeve, taking over the spinach, washing the leaves and pulling the rough stems so that Bridey might be tempted to eat some. "Only some few little things left to do."

"What did you end up using for wings?"

"Oh, wings," Maeve answered vaguely.

At the bitter, housebound new year, when there was nothing between Eimhear O'Halloran and the poison she was turning over in her mind, she snapped. It was not Maeve's Grammy brought the news this time. (Grammy'd had a bad December, and what none of them knew was that she wasn't going to last the winter, the news itself maybe delivering the final blow.) It was Father Gregory, who came to ask if Maeve's mother would help lay out husband and wife, seeing as Eimhear had been her dear friend for so many years. Of course, she agreed, but she first she had to leave the room and cry into her apron as none of them had ever heard her cry, for she'd never lost a child of them and hadn't even lost her mother yet, she was that unused to loss.

While he was waiting to accompany her mother to the farm, where the bodies still lay, Father Gregory sat shaking his head, not touching the tea Maeve had made for him on her Ma's instructions. Maeve's Da sat next him, the war within him over whether to console or ignore the priest plain on his face. Finally, he took a meaty hand and patted the Father's shoulder. A sob caught in the priest's throat.

"She never forgave him, I've no doubt," said Maeve's father, asking more than explaining.

"Yes, yes, it was losing the little girl drove her to it," nodded the priest. "But such a sin—murder and suicide! It's more than a body can compass, even with the comfort of Our Lord."

"Yes, Father, a mother's love is a fierce thing," said Da, squirming now he was obliged to hear the priest out.

"And the blood! A shotgun at close quarters, mind you. You couldn't have imagined the damage . . ."

But they hushed when Ma returned, her face scrubbed of tears and her apron changed for a clean one.

Maeve and her father were both low in spirits after they'd gone, though the boys were still young enough to enjoy the horror of the story and had to be told often to quiet down in their riotous play. Da sternly refused to inform Grammy, who was bedridden and called feebly for the news every few minutes. Finally, he sent Maeve upstairs to her grandmother, but with a cautioning: "Don't bring a word of her superstitious shite back to me, do you hear, Maeve-girl? And you're not to listen to it yourself!" As it happened, there was no need: Maeve's report so shattered the old woman that she lay like a dead thing, her faded eyes, grey with cataracts, glistening like those of a bird frozen out of its nest.

Maeve had her own opinion of Eimhear O'Halloran's deed, and it was that she didn't condemn Eimhear for anything but her timing.

When Maeve woke on Hallowe'en, she knew she'd been dreaming. The dream atmosphere was very thick around her, and it raised the hair on her head, it was that electric with fear. The anxiety of it trailed down the hall from the in-law suite with her, like ghost fingers that had become caught in her clothes and hair. She only felt free of premonition once she entered the kitchen to find a silvery autumn light streaming onto her little great-granddaughters, intent on their breakfast. There must have been something left in her face of the delight she felt on seeing the girls because, spotting her, they lifted their spoons together and chimed, "Grammy O'Neal, Grammy O'Neal, Trick or Treat, Trick or Treat!" until Shelly put her hands on her ears and told them please stop.

Maeve laughed, and said, "Whoosh, you'll wake the dead!" which made them fall silent with surprise. "Because it's Hallowe'en, you see," she added quickly, and that seemed to please them.

When Brian had taken them off to their schools, Shelly began collecting the dishes. Maeve put a hand on her wrist. "I'll do that, lovey. You'll be late for work."

Shelly seemed to hesitate for a moment, but she shook her head, taking the bowls to the dishwasher and reaching down to load them onto the lower rack. She didn't look at Maeve when she asked, "You still have those wings to make, don't you?"

Maeve sat down again heavily and closed her eyes, pressing the dread down inside her. When she opened them, it was to find Shelly emptying a plastic bag onto the table before her. "Yellow Submarine Costume and Novelty" was written across it in bright, dancing letters.

"I don't mean to interfere," Shelly said, sitting down beside her, "but you've done so much already. Why not use these?"

They were white satin angels' wings, not faeries', but they were spectacularly, glowingly, wings, nonetheless. They were to be pinned at the back and tied round the waist with white ribbons. They were cheaply made, yet each pair spread out boldly on its wire frame. There would be no hiding these wings from jealous eyes.

Once Shelly left the house, Maeve went to her room and stuffed the bag of wings in the back of her closet on the floor behind the box of Caoili's things which she kept for sentiment. Then she turned the blinds and lay on her bed in the dim light, rubbing her gnarly hands gently across her eyes again and again.

Frank was best man she had ever met. He had none of her father's morbid temper, and he laughed without malice. He'd come out for a visit with her cousin Aiden (they'd been chums at university) and stayed on, leasing a tiny crofter cottage a two-hour tramp from her parent's farm, writing a book there, a novel, he said. He had a legacy from his aunt that would last him until the book was finished, and then a teaching post waited for him at a school in Galway. He and Da hit it off right away, the two of them trading jokes about the Church until her mother and herself had to leave the room.

Though she'd two years on him, he loved her right on seeing her the first time. No one wondered how they felt about each other, herself and her Frank—it was clear from the moment they met.

They were married in July, and Caoilin came to them in April, and there was no worry whose she was—she had his gold hair and blue eyes. That autumn, they had their first and last argument over the baby. From the start, he'd teased her about the talismans and the prayers, but he only lost his temper when she was on him not to touch the child.

"She's mine, as well, Maeve O'Neal, and I will not have you dictate to me when and how I shall kiss my little girl!" He was flushed a furious red. She didn't know him then, he was that changed. And it was at that moment she realized he would never understand, never hear her, but he would turn into this thing she didn't know and lose her this baby and every baby she loved. They would lose them to the evil folk and have dummies for children all of their life together. She bit her lip until it bled, and he kissed away the blood and they forgave each other.

And because it was clear how they loved each other, when she did what she had to do, no one suspected.

Bridey was brought home before noon, eyes glazed from treats at pre-school—orange-iced cupcakes, she told Maeve with a wistful look. Erin burst through the front door at one o'clock—early dismissal, Maeve remembered, so the smaller ones could make their rounds before dark. The two were so giddy with expectation that they got Maeve's head spinning.

"All right, all right, that'll be enough, you girls!" she shouted above their noise. They were startled by her sharpness. "It's a good few hours until you'll be going to trick-or-treat. You'll have to wait for Mommy or Daddy, so there'll be no spoiling your beautiful costumes!"

At half-past two, hounded to distraction by their entreaties, Maeve got the costumes from the sewing room. She'd done the final touches late in the night, and neither little girl had seen her completed costume in all its glory. Both girls were awed into silence as she hung them off the backs of chairs for viewing. They ran to them and touched all the little trims, comparing details with each other, chirping and singing their excitement.

Once dressed in their finery, the little girls posed and spun and stared at themselves for a long time in the large mirror that covered one wall of the foyer. Maeve pinned up their hair and fastened the crowns on their heads. In the excitement of the dressing and the effect of the costumes, they'd not thought of wings.

She timed it for the beginning of week, when no one from the farm was likely to visit. She chose an hour when Frank was deep in his writing to slip into the woods, to a part of the forest she usually avoided because of the faerie rings. It took her just a few minutes to find them, the Death Caps, where they grew in frightening bunches on the dark side of trees. They were pale and long-stemmed as sickly men's things. She'd never had the inclination to touch them in the first place, even without the warnings from her Ma and Da, but now she steeled herself and gathered them into her apron, crossing herself over and over, in case these particular toadstools served as seating for one of the Evil Ones.

Coming home, she caught a glimpse of him through the window, working at the table, the lamplight setting his hair off so that it shone like her wedding ring, and she thought she wouldn't have it in her to do what must be done. He must have felt her eyes on him because he looked up and spotted her, his own eyes catching fire, so that she folded her apron over to hide the death she carried in it.

But then the baby cried, and he was first one up the stairs to the little loft room, snatching her out of her crib, cooing and carrying on like a daft person, and she set her jaw, pressing her hand on her heart to stop it shuddering.

That night she made a stew, adding all their bacon, thick with rind and coated in salt, to cover the taste, and chopping the caps very fine so that he wouldn't notice them. But she'd been right all along—a city man like Frank had no notion of toadstools, just as he'd no sense of the faerie folk.

"Frank O'Neal, I love you," she told him, clutching him even as he ate the stew, while Caoili, worn out with her father's foolishness, lay sleeping in her basket on a chair beside him. Afterward, they bundled themselves up and took a walk, as they did every night, unless it rained, with Caoili in the sling Maeve wore to carry her, and Frank picking late groundsel and sticking it in Maeve's hair and tickling the inside of her ear with long grasses, and kissing her.

When they had returned and put the baby to bed, she pulled him into the bedroom, undoing his shirt buttons and looking down away from his eyes.

"Why, shameless Maeve O'Neal, seducing me like this!" he said, lifting her chin and stroking her hair. They never even got as far as their underthings, the cramps came on him so fast. She was afraid he'd bring the poison up, but it stuck in him, and he was too wretched sick to leave the bed. She sat with him while he was out of his mind and babbling, holding his hand for long hours in the night and the next morning, even while she fed and dandled the baby with the other hand, and by afternoon, the first crisis was over and he smiled at her weakly, his pale face slick with sweat.

He started his dying on the third day. Whenever she could spare the moment from Caoili, she held his hand and wiped his brow. His eyes were puzzled in those last hours, and she wondered did he suspect her.

When he'd turned yellow and his water was brown, she felt that he was very near gone, and she brought the baby to him and let her twine her fat fingers in his hair. Then Maeve broke down and cried and cried and put her head on his chest, and told him everything, all about the jealous sheoque or spriggan it would have been who stole Sinéad O'Halloran and how she knew he could never learn not to admire his baby so, and she begged him to forgive her. But by then, he was no longer awake and was soon dead beyond rousing. She waited another hour to be sure, stroking and stroking his cheek. Then she put Caoili in her sling and set out for the farm.

It was killing hard to lose her Frank. But she'd no regrets, for that was how she saved her Caoilin, and the two of them were very close without having to make a show of it for others.

When Caoilin was nineteen, she met an American tourist and married him, and they brought Maeve to Illinois, where there were no faeries, so that when Americans carried on about their precious freedom, Maeve knew exactly what they meant. By the time

Caoilin's son Brian finished high school, the marriage was bad, but Caoilin separated from her bullying husband was even more beautiful and loving than before, so it was terrible when the cancer took her. No one should have to watch her child die.

It was turning dusk when the doorbell rang with the first of the trick-or-treaters. These were the littlest children with their parents and with baby sisters or brothers dressed as pumpkins or bumblebees because of their round figures. Maeve let the girls hold the bowl together while a father or mother guided a child's hand to the candy. The girls' eyes glittered. They were so pleased with themselves that they hardly took in the Little Mermaid or Spiderman or Harry Potter before them, but waited for the praise they knew to expect, Bridey at once eager to be seen and still shy enough to forget her dignity and let her thumb drift up to her mouth.

"Look at your beautiful dresses!" mothers exclaimed. The fathers wouldn't think to notice other children's finery, but made certain that their own little ghost or fireman or dinosaur thanked the girls politely.

"So what have we here?" One father squatted to be at eye-level with the girls. "Two . . . well, two . . ." He paused and his wife took over.

"They're ballerinas, Alan! Gorgeous ballerinas!"

"We *faeries*!" shrieked Bridey, giggling.

Erin bit her underlip and looked down at her own costume, and her eyes widened in horror. Maeve's heart began a frantic pulsing; she hurried the couple's little boy in choosing his treats. "We forgot the wings!" Erin wailed. The woman gave them a puzzled smile, as Maeve pulled the two girls back and closed the door. Erin ran before the mirror and stamped her foot at her image. "We forgot the wings! No one knows what we are!"

"We f'got wings, G'ammy," said Bridey, but she kept an eye on the door and listened for the bell. She was having too much fun to trifle over details.

Erin was furious. "Faeries have *wings*! I'm not going trick-or-treating without wings!" She pulled off her crown and flung it down the hall. Bridey's eyes grew large with fear; she looked from door to sister and back again. The doorbell rang. Erin scowled at the floor. A thrum of pain was making its way from Maeve's jaw to her temple.

The three of them started as Shelly entered the hall from the garage, laughing at something Brian was saying behind her. When the doorbell rang again, Erin sat down hard in front of the mirror and crossed her arms. Shelly trod on Erin's crown and stepped back in surprise.

A wave of nausea washed over Maeve, so strong that she teetered and propped herself against the wall. "Grammy?" said Brian as he went to her, catching her by the elbow and putting an arm around her back. Erin stood up and backed away toward her mother. "Get a chair from the kitchen!" Brian cried to his wife, bracing himself to support Maeve.

But Maeve turned her face from them so that she could see Bridey, who had gone to the heavy door and pulled it open with both hands.

"Trick or treat!" came the shout from a large group of children framed in the doorway. Maeve looked at the creatures gathered on the doorstep, the ones in front shifting uncertainly at the scene inside the house. Pain was stabbing at her head, and now the edges of things were rimmed with an eerie light so that the monsters and hags clustered at the door glowed dangerously. Then, as some faltered and retreated and others, unaware of the mayhem inside, pushed forward, she spotted it, one of the Evil Folk, a rat-faced far darrig, hairy and snouted. She watched in horror as it made its way to the front of the group where Bridey held out the bowl of sweets.

With a strength that came from God Himself, Maeve shook off Brian just as Shelly returned with the chair. She flung herself at Bridey, pulling the precious darling backward and pushing against the door with her hip to close it before the thing could reach them. In the silence that followed the slam of the door, she saw the look on Brian's face and took a step toward him, but her knees buckled and she fell before the mirror, hitting the floor with a sickening crash. The thin wail of the little girls came to her as from a distance, and Brian and Shelly also, crying out through mouths of treacle. She was aware of a burst of furious activity around her. Every bit of her was rent with pain.

But Maeve was at peace. She'd done it again, saved her girls. She looked into the glass where she lay, content to wait for the paramedics she knew would come for her. Even the knowledge that now she was surely bound for the nursing home had no power of despair over her. Peering into the mirror through the black fog that was eating into the edges of her vision, she caught her breath.

Why, there it was! The murderous Thing! It had got inside somehow with its contorted face and mad yellow eyes and twisted claws.

And as she tried to push it away, it reached out to her and pulled the breath from her body, and she slipped after it into the dark.

SETTLING ACCOUNTS

When Ralph Burton slipped behind the west wall bleachers to practice his valedictory speech for the Class of 1968, he surprised Amy Bradshaw, who crouched on the floor under the risers, stuffing her fist into her mouth to make herself stop crying. He winced to see her wipe mucus from her nose with the inside edge, the gold lining, of her Quakerton High robes. Her mortar board was lying on the floor amid the discarded candy wrappers and crushed plastic cups from the awards ceremony the night before. As he picked it up, some drops of cola or coffee beaded up along the top; he wiped it off against his pants leg and handed it to her. She gave him a weak smile. Ralph would have liked to slip away then, but he couldn't stand to see the way Amy's mascara had dissolved down her cheeks. Pity choked him, made him furious; he wanted to shake her.

"Here." He gave her the packet of Kleenex he was keeping handy in case he started to sweat at the podium.

Amy turned scarlet. "Thanks." She took a tissue and blew her nose loudly. "I don't have a mirror."

Ralph squatted and got a closer look. He pulled more Kleenex from the package and directed her to spit in it and wipe where the black ran in streaks from her eyes.

"That's it. You . . . look . . . great." He was talking through clenched teeth again, as he did when he was nervous or angry.

Amy shrugged off the compliment. "I can't go to State."

This was not what Ralph wanted now. He had specifically not asked for an explanation. He stood up.

"We were drinking Applejack at the quarry Sunday night—you know, me and Jason and Bill and Carly, and these state troopers just appeared out of nowhere. The other guys got away, but I was too smashed to move."

"So your dad's mad about that." He glanced out the open double doors at the west entrance to the field house. The seniors were starting to mass for the graduation processional.

Amy gave him a disgusted look. "Of course not. Old Dan doesn't give a shit what I do as long as it doesn't cost him any money." She went right on explaining, though he could tell the processional was going to start soon because the students were being directed to form lines. Right up front, of course, was Alvin Webster, second-in-the-class, fingering his salutatory introduction anxiously and probably hoping for a miracle that would keep Ralph from showing at all.

"That stupid Rotary Club found out. They took back my Good Citizenship Award. That's $50 for my books—" She started sucking up sobs again. "Where the hell am I going to get the money for books now?"

Ralph looked nervously at his watch. "I think we'd better get in line."

"You go. You're in the first section. I'm not until the hundreds. A hundred-and-fucking-five out of two-hundred-and-eighteen." The seniors had been organized according to class rank. The top of the class would fill the front row, with Ralph in the seat of honor. Amy buried her face in her hands.

Ralph set the remainder of the Kleenex carefully by her feet and backed away. He gave a last look before abandoning her completely. Amy was running her fingers through blond-streaked hair and wiping at her eyes with the tissues. Although every effort seemed to create more mayhem of her face, he told himself that she was getting it together now, that he could stop feeling bad for her, forget about her.

And he did . . . though once, only once, during his speech, he stumbled on the phrase "for each of us to realize a dream," thinking briefly of Amy Bradshaw sitting in the detritus of the award celebrations.

Ten weeks later, Ralph and his father entered the Stenholdt Feed Store together for the last time before he was to leave for college. For once, Ralph wasn't thinking about the way the rest of the customers got quiet or whispered to one another whenever the Burtons came in. He was thinking that he had to find a way to say goodbye to Sean Murphy, the boy he had silently adored for ten years, so that it would mean something important to both of them and still not give Ralph away.

Ralph had been eight years old, walking the south cornfields with his father to check for Stewart's Wilt, when they came upon the Murphys unloading their truck at the dilapidated Lewis spread, which had been deserted for decades and which would soon come to be called "the Murphy place," though it never got the face-lift it had coming to it after so many years of neglect. John Burton had pitched in right away, cheerfully helping the couple and their two adolescent girls settle in, though Ralph could read the worry in his father's eyes, even through the gentle enthusiasm he always generated. He thought about the ears his dad had stripped from a few of the stalks and stuffed into his overalls to take home and examine.

Emptying the truck of all the family's possessions was the work of a few minutes. They had shaken hands all around; Patty Murphy had invited them for coffee, and Ralph was inwardly wishing they could leave the sad little house with the useless broken porch and sagging roof. Just then, from around the back of the barn coop came a boy about his age, but smaller and better formed—beautiful, really, with deep blue eyes that flashed mischief and dark unruly hair that invited fingers to curl themselves in its locks. There was a lot of loud teasing, especially on the part of the boy's older sisters ("never around when there's work to do, Sean-boy!"), though Ralph noticed that they smiled and tousled his head a good deal. The beautiful boy ignored them, but held out for Ralph's perusal a battered Hopalong Cassidy lunchbox, which made Ralph blush for him—it was a baby's toy, something Ralph might have been proud of a few years earlier, but not now—until opening the lid, he disclosed contents of genuine wonder: a silken cocoon, a snake's rattle, three broken pieces of a of robin's eggshell wrapped gently in tin foil . . . From that moment, Ralph was in love with Sean Murphy.

The Murphys could not seem to prosper, and their attempt at farming failed within two years, in spite of John and Ralph hurrying across the fields to the warped and rotting saltbox farmhouse every day after their own chores. The father James Murphy was feckless and ran off soon after the farm gave out, and Patty got a job as a dental secretary in Grace Falls, twenty-six miles away, so it was Bea and Linny who raised, more or less successfully, the troublesome younger brother they adored.

The two boys were together as much as they could manage those early years, mostly outside or at Sean's house, where there was little to mess, but even less to eat, though the girls, when they were home, fussed over them as though they were champions. When they got hungry, they went to Ralph's and baked brownies in the wood-burning oven that appeared in the old photograph of Ralph's grandmother, which hung in the hallway with many more such records of the dead in his family. There was one of his mother dancing for the troops before they left for Europe; it never failed to move him because the side-seam of her costume was unraveling, revealing the elastic of her underpants, while her luminous face was so obviously ignorant of this exposure.

Summers were best because whenever they could catch an hour away from chores (not that Sean seemed burdened with these), they met for swimming. Blesswell's Creek had leeches, but also ropes hanging from the twisted limbs of trees. They were both brave, if only Sean was reckless, and they sent girls into squeals—and boys into hoots—of admiration as they threw themselves almost onto the opposite bank.

Best of all was a summer sleepover at Ralph's. Sean would hide a treasure downstairs in the darkened living room, which was so much more familiar during the daytime, when it was lit by a sun hostile to romance. He would choose the thing to hide from whatever box contained his collection at the time—a cigar box after the

Hopalong Cassidy and a tackle box during junior high, just before the treasure hunts stopped. (Later in high school, it would be a cashbox, where what he kept was mostly money, and weed.) Then he would draw a pirate's map with his finger on Ralph's bare back for Ralph to follow from the feel. Ralph would make him draw and redraw, not because he could visualize it better the second time, but so that the sensation of Sean's finger remained with him all during the search.

But when they started junior high, Ralph saw a lot less of Sean. They were split up for the tracking levels (Sean dropped two), and Ralph counted himself lucky to have Sean in homeroom for both seventh and eighth grades. They shared no extra-curricular activities—in fact, neither of them joined sports, though Ralph belonged to more than one school choir and entered every scholastic contest. Sean's interest was confined to girls, and to the auto-repair unit of shop. He was good at it, and earnest in a way Ralph had never seen him before, and the shop teacher Mitch Smithen was responsible for bailing Sean out of much of the trouble he attracted to himself.

By high school, however, without the mediating presence of Mr. Smithen, Sean seemed to spend as much time in detention as in class. And in this way, he and Ralph met up again.

All detainees were given the option of being tutored in any subject over the soul-deadening experience of strict detention. The most effective tutor on the team was Ralph, of course, not only because he was the smartest and could teach any subject, but because he could detach himself from the student, resist the temptation to talk and fool around. Then one afternoon, Sean Murphy waltzed into the room where Ralph had arranged his desk with protractor, compass, ruler, pencil and eraser in a neat row across the top, and presented his tutoring sheet to Ralph with a triumphant smirk: it was completely filled in—he had booked all of Ralph's tutoring times.

"Tutor me, tutor-man." He made a song of it, and they both laughed.

At first, Ralph was delighted. His greatest fear had always been that Sean would flunk out of their grade level and reduce to nothing the amount of time they saw each other. But he soon realized that Sean had no intention of spending these hours learning anything.

"You can't *guess* at the answer, Sean," Ralph said, clenching his teeth, trying to still the panic he always felt when Sean refused to focus on his work. "You don't *have* to guess: there are formulas to get you there."

Sean ducked his head as Louisa Bobbit entered the room, the lollipop she had stuck in the corner of her mouth in flagrant violation of the "no-food" policy in the tutoring room.

"Hey, check it out—Lucky Boob-tits!" Sean whispered. "Man," he moaned, "I need a piece of that." He dug in his jeans pocket and came up with a jawbreaker wrapped in cellophane. "I knew there was a good reason for saving this. She's always gotta have something in her mouth— know what I mean? Watch this!" He caught Louisa's wrist as she passed their desk on the way to the front row, where her tutor, acne-riddled Alvin Webster, sat in weary contemplation of his schedule, alternating sighing and looking at his watch.

"Oooh, Louisa, make me a lucky man," Sean whispered into her ear as she leaned toward him, a hand on her smile, squeezing her eyes closed in mirth. He dropped the jawbreaker into the breast-pocket of her blouse and ran his palm down her back to the waist of her mini-skirt, which he fingered playfully.

"Naughty, naughty boy, Sean Murphy," she laughingly shot back at him, loud enough to wake Alvin from his stupor of misery. Alvin pushed his glasses up his nose, looked at his watch again and scowled at Louisa as she continued up the aisle to her seat.

Finally, Ralph gave up, deciding to spend this precious time making himself happy by making Sean happy: he simply did Sean's homework for him, being careful not to get every question right, especially the hard ones. Sometimes, though, he felt ashamed about wasting tutoring time like this when he witnessed the determination, even desperation, that some students— like that slob Dan Bradshaw's daughter Amy, for instance—brought to their work with the tutors. But Sean was oblivious to Ralph's sacrifice of ideals. He settled contentedly into his tutorial schedule, cracking jokes, telling stories, confiding his loves and hates to his oldest friend and, (next to girls) his best audience.

As soon as he was old enough, Sean Murphy quit school to work for the Stenholdts. No one could figure out how Eric Stenholdt and his brother Luther stopped themselves from firing him, but Ralph knew that Jenny Stenholdt had taken him under her wing.

On that August afternoon, in the week before Ralph's departure for college, the feed store was crowded, as usual, with farmers, and the communal discussion changed direction depending on who entered and left. Once the Burtons had made their way to the counter, John Burton nodding and smiling at his neighbors as he passed them, pockets of conversation picked up again.

For as long as he could remember, Ralph and his father had induced the sudden quiet, the stifled coughs and the glances darting between the men. For as long as he could remember, Ralph and his father had been misfits in the farming community in which they had both been born and which was their heritage.

But not because Ralph was in love with a boy—at least, he didn't think that was it. He was pretty certain no one knew. But if the Burtons' neighbors didn't suspect he was queer, still, he realized that many of them wondered how he had turned out so . . . what? Sullen. Goony. "Wet," his classmates would have said.

Of course, there were those who thought it was to be expected, considering the woman John Burton married out of the USO in 1944, that singer/dancer from California. Most didn't remember Lena Burton, but fed their idea of her from a combination of images culled from film and television and exaggerated to cartoon-like proportion. Those who had loved her, however, remembered that she'd been a farm girl, too, before joining the USO. One of those had been Jenny Stenholdt, who couldn't have kids herself and had sat with John in the waiting room while Lena brought her son into the world and left it at the same time, a victim of a freak burst appendix which went undetected during the labor. But for most of the farmers of their small township, the fact that Lena Burton had been a showgirl went a long way toward explaining that odd boy of hers.

"So it's really going to be the big city this weekend, huh, Ralph?" Eric asked him from behind the check-out counter. He was playing with the Lab mix Babs, teasing her with a rawhide bone. "Guess they want you pretty bad. Your dad says you got a whopper of a scholarship."

Ralph and his father both lowered their heads shyly at the attention, though Ralph could tell that his father was pleased.

"Lots of 'em, Eric," put in Red Royer, Bobby Royer's father. "You should've seen him at the awards last June at the high school. Wore his soles out going up for them."

"I know that, Red. Jeez, Jenny has a goddam list on the cork board at home. What I meant was the college is giving him money, too. And he don't have to pay it back, neither."

"Yes," said Ralph quietly. "I'm very lucky to have it." In the past few weeks, the uneven stumps of three teeth in one side of Eric's mouth had made Ralph dizzy with nausea, though he couldn't remember a time when they hadn't been there.

"Got an even bigger one from SUNY, so Dirk Myers told us," said Jenny Stenholdt, Eric's wife. Until lately, she had been one of Ralph's biggest fans, always commenting on his awards when they were mentioned in the *Gazette*, even bragging about him to others as she rang up sacks of feed and seed corn. ("Heard what my boy Ralph did this time, Bill? Just won a national writing award for a paper on—jeez, what was it, Ralph? You tell him.") But since the school counselor Myers had told her that Ralph was going to NYU, instead of SUNY-Buffalo, she had cooled toward him. "Boy of mine would go to a state school with the kind of money they give you."

"Got to let them fly, Jenny," put in Ralph's father, beaming innocently.

A knot of farmers had formed in what Eric called his "showroom" and were fondling the new tools that had arrived on the truck that morning. These were men, Ralph knew, who agonized over every purchase, patching and taping gloves and clothes and roofs and barns, jerry-rigging washing machines and tractors and combines, until they could no longer hold out against the necessity to replace them. The image of Amy Bradshaw worrying away at her raccoon eyes with soggy Kleenex came to his mind. He shook it off.

"What's he need a scholarship for, Burton?" asked Blake Leemington. Ralph winced. He reminded himself that Leemington was not really hostile, just bewildered, like the rest of them. "You make plenty off that gourmet stuff of yours, don't you?"

John Burton laughed. "You can never make enough, Blake. You know that. Anyway, this is a merit scholarship Ralph won. It's just for doing well at school. It's not need-based."

Ralph winced at the word "need." What set Ralph Burton and his father apart from these men was that John Burton had beaten the odds, had found a way to turn his poor failing farm and orchards into a success, by becoming a provider of New York City restaurants and specialty groceries and delicatessens. He had even opened his own small store on the highway, selling high-priced produce, exotic preserved foods, and home-baked pastries and pies. The *New York Times* had done an article on him, with photographs of jars of "Burton's Red Wine Chutney" and "Burton's Champagne Peach Marmalade." The article identified several of John's regular customers as famous chefs, and though in the photographs they looked like all the rich tourists who treated the fields and farms and the little town as weekend curiosities, Ralph remembered the cosmopolitan aura and respectful interest these professionals brought with them.

"What're we going to do without you, Ralph?" asked Jenny, suddenly changing attitude.

"Oh, Jenny, oh, boys, there she's goes . . . oh, count on the women . . ." came from several of the men as Jenny rounded the counter to give Ralph a hug. It was clear the men enjoyed watching tough little Jenny Stenholdt go soft like that. She was short, bone-thin and hard, with nothing in her bra that could embarrass him, and a face weathered at least a decade beyond her thirty-eight years, but his back stiffened as it always did when someone put a hand on him. That didn't throw Jenny, though, and she clung to him until Babs dropped the rawhide and jumped up to be included, licking first Ralph's hand, then Jenny's elbow. They both laughed, pushing Babs off them.

"You lookin' for Sean, he's out back" she said, brushing away tears as she turned back to the counter. Ralph blushed and then hurried from the farmers and their testy camaraderie toward the back of the store.

"You be good that far away from home in the wicked city," Dave Missal called after him with a wheezy laugh. "Don't spend your old dad's money on loose women and LSD." There was a round of snorts and chuckles.

Ralph waved, as though he were leaving that instant, as though this were the last time he would see any of them, the last time his stomach would go queasy at the thought of Eric's teeth, and the sense of release seemed to lift his feet. But just before he slipped through the stockroom door to the loading dock, some small tug within made him glance back at his father, amiably fielding questions from the neighbors who had never forgiven him for what they considered his defection.

"He's always been a sound kid. I don't worry about Ralph," Ralph heard his father confiding to the group, as the door hissed closed behind him. His heart swelled with both fondness and irritation for the sweet little man. Ralph was a good son; he knew it himself. He had always worked hard, studied hard, hidden the guilty infatuation he carried with him for Sean Murphy every minute of his life since that dirty-faced sprite had opened his Pandora's box of woe for Ralph.

Outside the store, Ralph squinted against the sudden light, shading his eyes to locate his friend.

"Shit, Burton," Sean said when Ralph had spotted him and loped over. Rather than hauling feedbags or restocking hardware, the way he was paid to do, Sean was lounging against the rusted Thunderbird he'd got running earlier that spring. "I can't believe you're going," he complained. "I can't even think what it'll be like around here without you." Sean was not alone: he had one arm flung casually over his girlfriend Francine's shoulders, while Francine's younger sister glared at the two of them from inside the Thunderbird. Ralph knew how she felt.

The boys shook hands, Sean disentangling himself from Francine long enough to give Ralph a kind of half-embrace, the way men did with one another after some moment of shared glory or stifled emotion. Sean only came up to Ralph's nose, and Ralph closed his eyes and relaxed his back at the sensation as his friend's lips accidentally grazed his neck. Sean pulled away fast and, to cover his embarrassment, gave Ralph a punch in the side. There was an uncomfortable silence until, "Hey! I've got something for you!" Sean cried. He opened the driver's side door to the Thunderbird and reached in.

Ralph jerked with surprise, and his heart soared. Had Sean broken from the cell of his own self-absorption long enough to actually buy Ralph a farewell gift? The idea called up the welter of love Ralph had felt at the moment when the lunchbox had first offered its secret passage to Sean's soul.

When he emerged from the car, Sean had the scratched cash box he kept under the seat. "Hold this," he said, handing the box to Ralph and positioning his body to block it from the view of both girls while he worked the combination. Behind him, Francine gave Ralph an arch look, the corners of her mouth turning down.

When the tumblers fell into place, Sean lifted the lid and extracted something Ralph couldn't see. He snapped the lid shut, took the box from Ralph and dropped it on the front seat. Then, to Ralph's horror, he held three twenties up like a fan. Ralph backed away, pushing the air in front of him with both hands and shaking his head. Sean grasped one of Ralph's hands firmly in his own strong ones and crammed the bills into it, squeezing it closed until tears of pain came to Ralph's eyes.

"Take it, asshole!" Sean said, turning his head to look away. "You can't get laid if you can't pay." Francine giggled at this; her sister gave a disgusted grunt and looked at her lap.

Ralph felt a thrill of anger at the base of his neck, the kind that sometimes threatened to choke him. He gritted his teeth so hard that a stab of pain shot from his jaw to his temple.

Ten years of having his guts ripped out every time he saw Sean. Ten years of resisting the urge to write Sean's name in his journal. Ten years of watching Sue-Ellen Hanson or Sandra Mattelock or Bernice Switt let Sean feel their tits, and later, lick the ice cream from Sean's lips, and later still, slip their hands into his pants.

Ten years of longing for the return of a boy who lovingly wound strips of tin foil around the fragile blue remnants of shell. Waiting for the crass accretion of thoughtless lust and selfishness that had encrusted this boy over the years to fall away and reveal him innocent again, and Ralph's.

Ten years of this, and what was his reward? Three limp bills for a pop in a cheap hotel on Broadway. He was sick with hurt and anger.

Just then, Ralph's father turned the pickup into the lot and backed it up to the loading dock. Sean immediately detached himself from Francine, who had come forward to put her arm around his waist with an air of peevish ownership, and jogged to the dock to take the feed order from John Burton. Sean fetched the various sacks from their stations in the storeroom and around the lot, and Ralph and his father loaded the truck. John Burton shook Sean's hand, and then Ralph did the same, avoiding Sean's eyes. He climbed heavily into the pickup and drove his father back to the farm.

That Saturday, two hours into the ride on the Greyhound bus for Albany, Ralph jerked awake at the thought of Amy Bradshaw. He knew that at Albany he would have a change of bus and a forty-five minute wait. There he dumped his bags in a locker, first taking an envelope from the package of writing paper Jenny had given him as a good-bye present—Labrador retrievers adorned the margins, mugging in various good-dog attitudes, and the card had been signed by "Jenny, Eric, and Babs," though Babs was more mutt than Lab, as anyone could see. He asked the clerk at the ticket window for the location of a mailbox. He found it a few blocks from the terminal and, pressing the envelope against it, he wrote, "Amy Bradshaw, Bradshaw Farm, Route 49, County Line Road, Quakerton, N.Y." adding his own zip code hopefully. He pulled Sean's bills from the inner pocket of his wallet, where he had kept them, marked in the corners with blue ink so that he would not spend them, and sealed them in the envelope, which he dropped in the box.

As the bus drew away from the dock at Albany, Ralph found himself thinking of his calm, resigned father working alone, quietly and intently, at his chores. By this time (Ralph checked his watch), he would be stirring three or four pots of preserves and checking the pies. Ralph pictured him by the two stoves—the wood burner (finally converted to gas) installed by the grandparents he'd never known, and the new range and oven his father had bought that spring to handle the increase in baked-goods orders. The sun would be low, sending a weak glow onto the several layers of dull white with which the cabinets were painted, lighting their chipped glass pulls and dancing against the yellow gingham half-curtains and valance Jenny had sewn for his father and then replaced for him every few years.

He and his father had worked together side by side in that kitchen, in the fields and the barn, the orchard and the pens, all the years of Ralph's life. They had sweated and moved comfortably and lithely around one another and had said very little, but had meant everything they said. And yet no word had ever been spoken between them about Ralph's sexuality. The gentle man had never asked or wondered aloud about the lack of dates, the lack of interest in sports, the steady habits and careful ways of his handsome only child. But, thought Ralph, they were outcasts, both of them. There was no need for explanation.

He went back to sleep.

GIRLS WITH GUNS

I am halfway down the stairs to Gampa's root cellar when Steak hollers for me.

"Blink!"

Steak knows I won't raise my voice. So he knows he can't hear me down Gampa's cellar. I stop on the stairs and count my breaths, waiting to see does he mean to make me climb the halfway back up to answer.

"Blink!" Where's the goddam beer!"

If Bill-Moe Wiltshire and Sonny D weren't with him, my brother wouldn't call me back like that.

We keep the beer in the root cellar, but summers when Gampa was alive, rutabagas and squash and carrots exploded out his garden, and he stowed them down the cellar, spread across shelves like great big jewels, spilling over baskets, like treasure, shining in the light of the one bulb strung to the ceiling. They looked warm 'til you touched them. We'd press them cool and smooth across our eyes for the headache or on our cheeks when the sun turned us red. They lasted all fall and into winter without canning. This is the truth. I hardly speak a word to people, but when I talk about the root cellar, they believe I am making lies of whole cloth, sewing tales, like our Gampa always said of his son, our daddy. But I don't lie. I don't say much, but I don't lie.

It's just beer down there now, PBR or The Beast, the bottles catching the light, or when it's cans, like some giant's teeth gleaming at me.

"Blink!"

So the beer has to wait while I climb back up to the living room where Steak and the friends he says are like brothers to him are watching Girls With Guns or More Girls With Guns or Girls With More Guns, all six boots on Gampa's burl maple coffee table already marked by sweaty bottles with rings-hooking-rings, circles and ghost circles.

They are no brothers to me.

"Jesus, Blink. Where the fuck's the beer?" Steak lets his mouth go round and stupid, being me. He's playing it up for Sonny to admire him.

"I was getting it, St—" I start, but Bill-Moe puts a hand to his ear to show he can't hear me, I talk so soft. "Eh? Eh?" he says, and he rolls around hugging his belly and yucking like nobody heard that one before. He makes little yips in his laughs, like Steak's girl Lu used to make when Steak was pushing in her.

Sonny stretches his mouth in a smile, the flat kind where you don't see teeth.

"I'm—" I start over, but my brother cuts me off, winking at his boys to show he's laughing with them, at me.

"Yeah, yeah, my girl, we know. We're just messing with you."

I turn away fast, but not fast enough, and they can hear me—blink blink blink—for every time that I close my eyes, holding my voice back in my throat, trying to swallow it before it comes out. That sets them hooting again. I start back down the stairs, pressing the sides of my head to still myself, singing in my mind, Over the river and through the woods to Gampa's house we go. "Here they come, boys," says Sonny. The laughing stops with a big suck of air. "That's what I'm talking about," he says, and I know some Girl with Extra Big Guns got their attention, and I go for the beer.

My daddy was the one named me Blink when I was twelve and Mumma died. That's the first time it happened—me having to say the word the same time I did it, like a twitch. Back then, we lived in the old house that came to Mumma from her family. I heard them from inside my bedroom. I heard them fighting down the hall, heard him strike her so hard she went quiet. Heard when he dragged her to the top of the stairs. I crawled on my belly out my room and alongside the second-floor banister in time to see him push her. And I watched her through the turned rails, running my finger hard along a groove, working a splinter into it and not caring to stop myself. One arm flopped out and in, out and in with each roll she took, like she was waving good-bye, and I had to close my eyes at each wave, and the word came out—blink blink blink—but too low for him to know I saw. She was so full of liquor, nobody thought a thing about it. Nobody thought that maybe she had some help dropping off this life into the other.

I'd always been quiet in a house with yelling. Doesn't talk much, people said. Still Waters Run Deep was Gampa's opinion. "You get lost in thought, Amelia," he said, but like it made him proud. Lost in thought, like thought was a place—the woods, or a city with lots of streets, where you would have a hard time finding your way home. But that would mean you want to get home.

I kept even quieter after Daddy killed Mumma because I knew he would go for me if I talked. But I was crying so hard at the funeral, I couldn't stop a hailstorm of blinks, and Daddy so mad at me I thought he might send me to Glory there and then.

"My girl, you quit acting the fool in front of everyone!" he spit. But his eyes slid to the faces on the minister and his wife, and he pushed out a laugh. "Aw, we'll have to give you a new name. Another baptizing, I'm thinking, Reverend. Put her in the water and she'll come up Blink." He turned his eyes on my brother. "That so, Bobby-boy?" And my scared little brother, meeting that crazy smile, nodded and nodded and let loose a turd in his pants. And then Daddy bent his face to the grave and made crocodile tears over our mother.

So, I got quieter still, and people stopped calling me shy, decided the right word was slow. Even some that liked me wondered out loud if I had two brain cells to strike a spark against each other. Sometimes it seemed they were right because once my mouth joined my face, from then on, I couldn't not do it and say it at the same time, and pretty soon it was so for Yawn and Sneeze and even Frown, if I found myself troubled enough. (But hardly ever Smile, because, like Mumma used to say, life is a Scotch miser when it comes to reasons to rejoice.) So if I have to speak, I keep my voice real low, in case one of these steals out and gets me the kind of attention I am tired of knowing.

I'm deep in the cellar, but I hear Bill-Moe say to the TV, "Will you look at that! Shit!" Like Lu always said, Bill-Moe's got a voice like a fingernail on blackboard and a face like the back end of a horse, but I keep that to myself and let the boys paint me foolish, instead. And I don't tell my brother how the other two spite him to his back. He thinks they named him Steak because he's tough like a bull, and he never lets me or anyone (even Lu, when she used to come around) call him anything else. But I heard Sonny once, when Steak was in the toilet, saying my brother was a dumbass with nothing but meat between the ears.

Sonny and Bill-Moe work metal with Steak at Beane's Ductworks in Brownsville, where our daddy ran a press when he was alive and sober. They spend the days cutting the sheets that Steak specs and they spend the nights at Gampa's house drinking Steak's beer and watching the same three DVDs of Girls and Guns over and over. They all want girls in bikinis like the ones in the DVDs, and they all want the guns, automatics. But all they have are the shotguns they set across their legs when they watch. Pump-action, except Steak's single-shot that belonged to Gampa, like everything else in the house. Sonny's is a sawed-off that he cut too short and illegal. (That's something you could crack on, how Sonny's so runty, so sawed-off, himself. But nobody says so.) He says he likes a big shot-spread, throwing his scrawny arms out wide, the skin sucked up into his ribcage over a little ball of gut. He never wears a shirt, and the tattoo he got in Greensburg State Prison goes right across the front of him from wrist-to-wrist FUCK WITH ME I FUCK WITH YOU. (I don't think he meant for it to be so, but when his arms are down, all you can see clear is ME I FUCK.) Big spread, he says. Wide scatter. He says he likes to do the maximum damage, and Steak and Bill-Moe nod, but I don't see where any of them get the time to shoot guns, when they are always in our living room, drinking and watching, until they fall asleep on the chairs and the couch and wake and grunt and curse the morning.

It's been one week four days since Lu took her last crack at getting Steak to drop his boys. I sat on the cellar stairs halfway down to hear her try.

"You're wasting your pay and your time on those bottom-feeders, baby, and I'm not hanging around to watch them pull you down. It's them or me."

You'd wonder how anyone could see two limp-hair, green-teeth, pasty-skin weasels past the light that girl gave off, never mind she's not as pretty as some, even me, probably. I had to press my head when the front door slammed behind her and started me blinking. The worst thing Steak ever did was let Lu go.

There was the time Gampa pulled Daddy from Parks' Tavern to shake him for begging money off Gampa's friends in Gampa's name, and the time Daddy burned our barn for the insurance money, but it looked like he was just what they call Gross Negligent, and that kind of stupid wasn't covered. But the time Mrs. Reverend asked me what happened to Bobby's eye and I couldn't speak to answer because God hates a liar, that was the straw that broke the camel's back. She marched me and Bobby and Mumma to Gampa's house right from church, and the three grownups sent us kids to play in the root cellar while they talked in the kitchen. I took gourds and apples and cabbages and made a castle around the two of us. Bobby wouldn't stop crying, so I sang the song, making it sound like neighing at The horse knows the way. And we stayed all night in Gampa's house with Mumma, while Gampa went to find Daddy to give him a piece of his mind. It had to be a tough piece to choke down because they didn't ever talk to each other after that. But we didn't feel Daddy's belt again until Gampa was gone.

The straw that broke the camel's back, Gampa called it, and I asked him later was it the same camel that couldn't fit through the eye of the needle to get to the Kingdom of Heaven? And he said, "Yes, Amelia." (He was dead before I was Blink, but my Gampa'd never call me something spiteful, anyhow.) "Yes. And can you imagine how hard it is for a camel with a broken back to fit through that needle's eye?"

By the time Gampa got sick, Daddy and him were taking care not to step in each other's shadow at all. One would cross a street not to meet the other. That meant no more family times at Gampa's house. Still, Mumma wasn't drinking anything harder than iced tea yet, and she backed us going over there on our own. When Gampa got too weak to stand, I took care of the garden and the cellar for him and brought up cukes and crooknecks to put on his fever.

The thing that'd been eating Gampa from the inside out finally gobbled up more than it takes to keep a body going. Daddy didn't permit us to go to the funeral, and he paid the Parks twins to board up Gampa's house, but he was still so scared of the old man, even in his grave, that he didn't dare sell it.

Without Gampa, our Mumma didn't amount to enough of anything to stand between Daddy's black temper and us. I think that's why she started drinking liquor, nicking a touch of Daddy's Wild Turkey when he wasn't looking, tipping it into the sewing thimble belonged to her great-gamma that she wore on a silver chain around her neck. It wasn't long before she stepped up to teacups and juice glasses and then just glugged it right out the bottle. Daddy was too drunk most of the time to notice, but if he did catch her at it, you never knew would he laugh and throw an arm around her waist and pour it down her throat for her, or beat her over it. And, of course, the last time he found her with his bottle, she went down the stairs, waving and waving good-bye, and I learned to blink.

After we buried Mumma, the times when Daddy wasn't right in the head got to be a bigger bite out of each day. He talked evil and wild about the people at Beane's Ductworks, who kept him on for our sake. And once, we came home from school to find him at the bottom of the stairs on his knees, like he was praying. Bobby pulled me back out the front door before he could feel us behind him, but not before I heard him pleading with something that wasn't there to forgive him. He got so he couldn't use the stairs at all or stand to see them even, and he started running out on us for weeks at a time, and that was fine with us.

Then one day, when we were raw and jumpy with expecting him to show, the sheriff knocked on the door. He had a woman deputy with him, and she took me in the kitchen to tell me what the sheriff was breaking to Bobby in the living room.

She held my hand for comfort, and I was ashamed how ragged I gnaw my nails. "Your daddy's dead," she said, and I wondered how she could look like an angel in that uniform. Don't blink, I told myself, don't. But there was nothing my face wanted to do then, it was empty for the first time in years. She told me how our daddy got hit by a truck away down in Tennessee. She didn't give too many details, but it was clear in my mind like I'd been right there when he wandered out the roadhouse and onto the highway in the dark, swearing and pleading with the people in his head and missing the rain and the lights and the sound of the tires that came for him. Nobody ever found out was he just blind drunk, as usual, or half-beat-up to begin with. But he was always so bothersome wherever he went that I figure somebody'd been teaching him a lesson.

I get scared I'm going to Hell for what I felt when my daddy died. Even Bobby cried. But then I remember the minister's face when he preached Daddy into the ground next to Mumma, how I knew he knew what Daddy was and that the world's heart rose up light once he was gone. It was the minister helped us sell the house where our mother died and got the church to fix up Gampa's, which was small, but fit us like a hug, so we could live where Daddy'd been afraid to step foot. I'd just turned eighteen and kept house for so long the State of Pennsylvania decided I could manage the both of us. The day we moved into Gampa's, I touched every spot I knew from being a little girl in that house. Touch touch, I whispered, knowing I was safe. The first couple years, I coaxed some pattypan and pumpkins, the prettiest squashes, out of Gampa's old weedy garden and put them down the cellar.

We had the money from Mumma's, and Mrs. Reverend got me the job mending clothing donations at the Loaves and Fishes Thrift Store that was run by the church. I worked in back, where hardly anybody saw me and I could Be Still and Run Deep most of the time. The Thrift Store was where we first saw Lu, who was picking through the jeans when Bobby came for me after school. Lu came out the washroom where you could try on what you were thinking of buying, and she flipped that yellow hair back over her shoulder and twisted to check her butt in the mirror. And never mind he never met her before and didn't even know her name, Bobby couldn't stop from saying, "Look at you." We always went for Blizzards on the way home from my job, and this time I told Lu I'd spring for three of them if she wanted to come with us. I didn't ever want to see that light leave Bobby's face that it had when he looked at Lu.

Sometimes I think about how for three whole years, me and my brother got to live every day in that little house where I first felt safe enough to take a full breath. I didn't know then that when our daddy staggered out in front of that semi, he'd already locked Bobby up and chucked out the key. Still, I may not be sure what happy is, but I think that's what we were, even after Bobby quit school, where there wasn't ever anybody on his side anyway, and started working steel at Beane's. We were happy right up until he came home with his new friends and his new name.

I stay out of their way, and except for their mean mouths, mostly they leave me alone.

And except for the other day, when Sonny D was stumbling for the toilet the same time I was passing the bathroom door and he pulled me in with him and turned the lock. He looked surprised as I was, so I figured he was too full of beer to know what he was doing, but when I reached for the doorknob, he took ahold my wrist and pulled me over with him to the toilet. He unzipped and one-hand aimed his stream at the bowl, and when he was done, it looked like he favored a wide scatter there, too. When he put it away, he didn't zip back up.

"Now it's your turn, my girl," he told me, turning me around to face him, pushing his naked little chest into me, my back to the toilet. I thought about the tattoo words in that hateful promise, them touching me like that, and I jerked my head away.

"But I'm not . . . I don't want . . ." I whispered so low he didn't understand.

"That what your brother calls you—My Girl? Right? What? . . . What's that?" He made his voice softer and pulled me tighter to him. "My Gir-ir-irl," he sang it like the song.

I didn't tell him no, it wasn't anything but Amelia that Steak called me when his boys weren't around. But I started to blink.

"That all you every say, girl?" he asked, breathing close, hot and sour. "Aw, don't you have something else for me, sweet girl?" He took my hand and stuck it in the opening of his pants.

"Blink! Blink! Blink!" I was choking out blinks too big and dry for my lazy throat, and the sound made him let go my wrist and back up.

"Shit!" he said, holding up his hands. "What the fuck's wrong with you?"

When I moved for the door, he grabbed both my arms. "Why don't you try another word, baby, see how it goes?" He put a hand on the back of my neck and squeezed. "Like maybe lick," he said, and he put his tongue on my face, "or—or . . ." He reached into his pants and took out his thing, which was showing a lot of interest in me. "Suck."

"Sonny, man!" My brother was knocking on the other side of the door. "You fall in?"

Sonny frowned. "Just a minute!" He pushed me aside to open the door. He flung it wide, so Steak saw me by the toilet, twisting my hands and moving my eyes and mouth together, and Sonny with his zip down. Steak's face was a question, but Sonny squinted at him, asked, "What?" low and full of poison, like he didn't need an answer.

Steak looked away. "Nothing," he said.

Sonny grunted and zipped up. "That's what I thought," he said, pushing through the door past Steak, who just let him pass. Steak stood aside the door, hanging his head, while we heard Sonny take the stairs down two at a time.

I supped up a last blink and said "Steak," stepping to him. But he scrunched his eyes and made a sound like the wind through something empty. Then he followed Sonny.

Steak is the way he is because of our daddy. I say Pinch to remind me so, whenever he loses the right idea of us. Pinch on the same spot on the inside of my arm, so there's always something there, black-and-yellow-and-blue, to remind me, we're both what we are because of Daddy.

So that's why, when I bring their beer and Sonny tells my brother to hand me Gampa's gun, I'm not surprised Steak does. And it's why I take the gun from him. Even if Gampa didn't teach me since I was six, I would know how to hold a gun from not being blind and having those DVDs for background to every last second of my waking life. But I pretend I don't know, let it hang down, pointing at the floor.

"Now we got our own Girl With Gun!" Bill-Moe whoops and starts up laughing. But Sonny has slit eyes, and I feel like there's nothing between me and what he's thinking. "Ain't she cute," Bill-Moe chokes out between yips, "our own little Girl With Gun?"

And it could go the way things tend to mostly, with me spending the rest of the time hiding in the cellar until the boys are wasted or wander off. And Steak sometimes shambling down the stairs when they're gone, bringing me Saltines and peanut butter the way I like them, like we were still kids together.

Or when it used to be Lu showed up, it was all I Don't Know How You Stand It, Amelia, Those Fools, talking the fret out of me, even though I couldn't ever explain to her about Daddy's tongue and Daddy's belt and the boy Bobby was and might have been because there's no way so many words, even if I could find them, would get past all the blinking to make sense.

It could go that way, Steak and me together, or Lu taking my side and stirring up a backwash of blinks. But that's not what happens this time.

"Ain't she cute?" Bill-Moe asks over and over.

"That's enough," says, Steak, but more like a question.

"Not yet," says Sonny. "She's still got her clothes on. Take your clothes off, Blink."

It's late in the day, and the sun is doing that thing with the motes in the air that I can remember all the years of my waked up life in Gampa's house. It breaks your heart the way a place keeps going on in its habits, changing light and soft breezes and the smell of woodsmoke and pine bark, like evil didn't just enter the room.

"I said take off your clothes, you stupid bitch."

I don't move, except Blink I say and do, blink blink blink. But nobody laughs. Steak comes toward me, but Sonny raises his sawed-off and my brother freezes. The blinks are coming fast and hard now, and I have to concentrate on what is going on around me to hear over my own voice, to see through those itty-bitty blackouts. They are so speeded up, everything looks like in an old-time movie. Jerky, but happening.

"Sonny, man." Steak laughs thin and wheezy. "What're you doing?"

"Let's see her in her panties, with that gun." Sonny's looking hard at me, but talking to Steak. "Like Bill-Moe says, our own little Girl With Gun." There's a click, and I know his safety's off. He pumps the sawed-off when he barks, "Shut the fuck up!" It takes a minute for me to know he's talking to me, that I'm still blinking out loud. And I can't stop, but make myself blink quieter, barely moving my mouth, my eyes slipping to my brother. Steak's face is red, his hands are making fists. Bill-Moe looks at the floor. Nobody's watching the Girls or Guns, but the light from the TV is still chasing around the room.

"Blink, baby, take it off," Sonny says. "Take it off, Blink." He starts stomping. "Blink! Blink! . . ." and I can't help it, my blinks follow the beat, coming right after his.

"Quit calling her that!" Steak screams, high and jagged, like cloth ripping, and everything gets tight. I quick drop my jeans and pull off Gampa's lumberjack shirt and the tank underneath it, shuffling the gun from one hand to the other. I don't bother with a bra most days, and this is one of them, and I see them all seeing me in my underpants. Just plain ones, just 100 percent cotton whites from the Walmart.

"That's better," says Sonny. "Now lift up that gun."

"Put your clothes back on, Amelia," my brother tells me, and I know they can hear the tears in his throat.

"Her name's Blink," says Sonny.

"Call her that again, you asshole!" Steak hisses at him. "Call her Blink again!" And he reaches for the gun I'm still holding, but Sonny's got the sawed-off ready and he fires, shooting one-arm so that it pulls wild away from Steak and me and makes Sonny lose his balance. The sound splits my head and bends me over and puts Steak to his knees, and even when I shake it off, my ears squeal.

Like Sonny always said, there's a big spread—just like his whiz—and a lot of damage, but maybe not the maximum because it dropped Bill-Moe, but missed Steak and me. Bill-Moe is twisting, clutching at his face and coughing strange.

"Shit!" says Sonny, and once he's got his footing back, he lifts and racks his gun.

But I say Shoot and do it at the same time, raising, aiming, releasing the safety and pulling the trigger smooth like Gampa taught me. The kick puts me on my ass, and the tight knot of shot puts Sonny down. He falls backward, his ropey little arms spread wide with their threat opened out for us to see. The sawed-off flies away out of his hand.

Bill-Moe's moaning, and I know it the second my brother sees that his friend is blind because he takes the gun from me and wipes it with the end of his Tee and puts his own hands all over it. Then he pulls me to my feet. "Put your clothes on, Amelia, and get in the cellar. I'm calling 911." His eyes slide to Bill-Moe. He talks slow and clear. "Sonny went crazy. He went crazy, Amelia." He looks at me, and I am not blinking. "He shot Bill-Moe." That's when I open my mouth, but he shakes his head. "I shot Sonny before he could shoot me. Say it, Amelia."

Back when Daddy broke the camel's back, I asked Gampa does God hate Daddy because he is a liar? There are the lies God hates, Gampa said, and the lies you tell for love. God hates the why, not the lie.

"You shot Sonny, Steak," I say, pulling on my jeans and bunching the rest under my arm, heading for the stairs to Gampa's cellar.

"You were scared. Ran to the cellar to hide out."

"I ran to the cellar, Bobby."

Bobby puts a finger on my cheek. I take his hand and say Kiss and do that. Then I start down the stairs.

HINDSIGHT

Meyer Kagan knew he had lived too long when everyone reminded him of someone else. He had always been able to recall the precise moment in his childhood when he realized that what made two people resemble each other was not height and hair color, but the composition of certain facial features. This awareness came to him when he was ten at the moment that he discovered in the face of his fifth-grade teacher the pop eyes, dimpled chin and cupid mouth of the actress Elsa Lanchester as she appeared in "Bride of Frankenstein." And because he remembered this moment exactly as he remembered learning to tie his own shoes, he saw it as a stage in his development.

The next step in Meyer's growing ability to connect faces involved recognizing the resemblance between two ordinary people in his life—a young woman at the circulation desk of the public library and his Uncle Eli's new wife Miriam. They should not have looked like each other at all, having different builds, complexions, styles of dress. But it struck him so forcefully, this resemblance, that for years, even after he had been promoted beyond the junior high school, he continued to expect the librarian's hushed voice when his vigorous aunt opened her mouth to speak.

He might not have registered the subtle next stage in the progress of this development but for the grinding of his mother's teeth when he remarked, "Doesn't Dad look like the President?" Both of his parents had voted for Roosevelt, so the only explanation for his mother's displeasure was that the man was not Jewish. And that is how Meyer Kagan became aware that he had crossed the race barrier. From that point on, the connections knew no bounds: cross-generation, cross-gender, cross-species (as it should surprise no one, since it is a known fact that dogs often look like their owners).

What Meyer could not remember was when it first occurred to him that he had a uniquely sensitive eye for resemblances. This was not always something to rejoice in. There were times, notably the period just before his retirement to the assisted living facility where he now found himself, that it caused trouble. Especially, he irritated his older daughter's husband Tom during the baseball playoffs, when he continually interrupted the television to make observations like, "I know who that batter reminds me of—it was a friend of Sheila's mother." He would cock his head in the direction of the kitchen to call, "Sheila! Get in here! . . . You know, they came every year for the theater season . . . Come here and look at his profile . . . Look! See what I mean?"

Usually, Sheila didn't see. Neither did Tom—or the kids. Meyer's grandchildren would tease him, even in public, asking with heavily contrived innocence, "Doesn't he remind you of someone, Grandpa?" And following this with giggles.

But the fact was, he saw more—or was distracted more by—such resemblances than other people. And he was beginning to feel haunted. No one looked like himself anymore. Meyer suspected that he had lived so long that he had used up all of the types of faces in God's repertoire. Who would have thought that there was a limit on that kind of thing?

Every morning in his breakfast nook, he carefully cut out all of the photographs from the newspaper with an X-ACTO knife so that he would not be distracted by resemblances while reading. The cleaning woman the girls had hired since the retirement of his housekeeper Mrs. Chin must have commented on his behavior to Sheila because he felt a tightening of his older daughter's scrutiny. He canceled the paper.

Then he really frightened his younger daughter Rachel, so much so that she told Sheila—always a mistake—and he was moved from the bungalow, his home for almost twenty-five years, to the assisted living facility Asphodel Estates.

At the time of his lapse, he was visiting Rachel in her flat in Portland, still wondering at the quiet resourcefulness his shy one had shown when her marriage broke up—what was it?—ten years earlier, was it that long? She had not remarried. Of course not, Sheila said with contempt, men just didn't know how to appreciate Rachel. Meaning Rachel was ugly—a sneer (though subconscious, he was sure) directed at both of them, Rachel and himself, since everyone knew that Rachel looked like him, just like him.

Even though associations were occurring to him with a disturbing intensity during this time, he had already stopped being a bore on the subject. Very early, he had learned never to tell people to their faces who it was they resembled. Often, when he thought the comparison a kind one, they were offended. Then, when he saw how

Sheila dropped her impatience for a new watchfulness, keeping these thoughts to himself became a matter of downright self-preservation: she was looking for signs of senility, of course, so that she could move him from his bungalow, the last place on earth where he could have his own way in everything. He stopped finding resemblances, or stopped talking about them, even around Rachel, whom he trusted.

But he slipped when he was visiting Rachel and the two of them were watching an episode of that frantic British comedy from the '70s. He had never understood the point of most of it, but he enjoyed the actors' good humor, the way they threw themselves into every skit. And it made Rachel laugh. She was beautiful when she laughed—he wasn't the only one who said so.

All of those young men in the program looked like someone else, but there was one—that Palin fellow. Meyer even asked Rachel the man's name because he knew he had seen that face clearly and often. It was an extremely familiar face. A famous face, he thought. Then in one scene, Palin appeared in muttonchops and wearing a Victorian frock coat, and even though the sideburns were red and Palin was a short man and only in his twenties or thirties at the time, Meyer knew him instantly.

"Abraham Lincoln! Don't you think so, Rachel? He looks just like Abraham Lincoln! Not in the portraits, but between shots, when he asked Mathew Brady if he could stretch his legs." Meyer chuckled. "Lincoln added, 'As if they could be longer!' Maybe he thought he had to beat Brady to such an obvious punch line. Lincoln loved a joke. But you should have seen the look on Brady's face . . ."

He trailed off. Rachel was staring at him.

Later, he tormented himself imagining the conversation between his two daughters: Rachel asking her sister tentatively if he had ever shown any interest in reincarnation, if he would ever believe in such a thing. It would be just the opening Sheila was waiting for, and she would pounce, cross-examining poor Rachel until she had the whole story from her, pressuring Rachel until she agreed to move him to a Home.

One small slip, and now he was paying for it. Now he was paying. He had a tiny efficiency with one window that looked out on nine months of constant cold rain, a prospect that could be charming if it included his own backyard with wrought iron café furniture on irregular and mossy patio tiles. Instead, he was faced with gray cement slabs punctuated by aluminum benches and cheap potted cedar trees. As for the flower tubs, not only were they not covered, but they still contained the blackened and spidery remains of the previous summer's ornamental plants.

It was here that they had moved him—to a place of unexercised minds and regulated meals, of over-familiar paramedical and uninterested janitorial staff. It didn't matter that he was still asked by his old department to teach a senior seminar from time to time—his daughters thought his mind was going. It didn't matter to them that he could still drive his own car from what he called As-For-Dull Estates, backing out of his space in the lot where a stream of the doddering and the wheelchair-bound made its way into the squat medi-van for an afternoon of shopping at a local mall. Such excursions were overseen by the obese senior nurse Christy, whose pallid baby face had a long history of resemblance in his mind—to a queen, a Brueghel peasant, a serial murderer, an actor, a waitress, a Pro-Life demonstrator and a secretary at the Education Department.

For that had been another, much earlier development, and one he once delighted in—the lineages of resemblance, or even the contemporaneous clusters. And the resulting triangles, in which two people who looked like the same third person did not resemble each other at all. He had a friend and colleague who had always reminded him of Jean-Paul Belmondo and David Letterman. Of course, a lot depended on how they moved. People watching his home movies always confused Sheila and Rachel, even though it was clear from the still photographs that they didn't look like each other at all. And of course, Rachel's laugh was her own, not his.

There was a woman at his table who looked like both Carol Channing and Eartha Kitt. That was what made her tolerable. And that her name was Sadie. But here, in the town where he had moved his girls after their mother died, three thousand miles from their birthplace, forty-eight miles to the nearest synagogue, you couldn't just slip into Yiddish because you sat at a table with a woman named Sadie. It was a measure of how far he had strayed from his own identity that these were the descendants of pioneer Sarahs and Sadies.

Of course, everyone spoke a little Yiddish these days. He got a charge out of hearing these flat-faced women try "meshuga" and "schmooze." They got it from television. He didn't own one, but he didn't object to watching with Rachel, whose taste in videos and programs always held a surprising pleasure. And he liked baseball, or used to. But now, all television alarmed him because everyone, almost without exception, reminded him of someone else. Because the people they resembled, like Lincoln, extended deep into the past, beyond his own past, to an intimacy he could not possibly have known.

To make matters worse, as he had grown older and the blows of life had accumulated, the number of faces that brought him pain had increased. For instance, there was a Korean anchor on one of the Portland stations who looked like his wife's younger brother Dutchy Goldstein, the poor boy. He had infuriated everyone when he was alive, everyone but Joanna, who adored him, but now the smooth, childish face of the news anchor brought back in a flash Dutchy hanging from the bars of his cell in Breakstone, Kentucky as vividly as if Meyer himself were there. Meyer couldn't bear to look at the face.

There were faces from the War and his very small part in it. There were faces that had lost children. Faces of schizophrenics; faces full of self-loathing. Faces dumb with anguish; faces disfigured by grief. Now that his skill transcended time itself, his lifetime, he was prey to faces, famous and anonymous, from the whole history of human cataclysms: faces from the Somme, from the Potato Famine, from the Reign of Terror, from even the Sack of Troy. And there were faces from hundreds of other sites of suffering too personal for him to identify: a black female face convulsed in sorrow—a modern-day Tutsi? A plantation slave? Some forgotten mother in some hopeless corner of the world now or ages ago.

It became a matter of utmost importance to limit his range of activities so that his exposure to new faces was reduced. Even the few daily familiar ones still held the possibility of new layers of identity, as his mind seemed to roam the temporal and spatial dimensions of the planet for connections. He dreaded the day when Sadie hurt him too much to look at.

But there were two faces he actually sought. For the first time in many years, he began to watch for his Joanna. After she died, he had purposely put himself in the way of people who reminded him of her, even going so far as to deliver a paper on women's suffrage—well outside his area of expertise—for a conference in London because of the slated appearance of a prominent British social historian as panel moderator. Based on the few flyleaf photographs he had seen, the feminist looked very much like a younger, darker, graver version of Joanna.

He would never know—the famous academic was a no-show, and soon after this, his desire to see his dead wife's face in the faces of others waned. But at that conference he managed to impress a history chair from the northwest college where a year later, at the age of fifty, he found himself applying for a professorship. Remembering the chair at the time of his application, he had the impression she looked like David Ben-Gurion (though her name was O'Donnell) and took that as a good omen, so that, once he was offered the position, he moved his family west, abandoning the climate of associations that was making his loss more and more unbearable. That this would be seen by the fifteen-year-old Sheila as a further betrayal (the first being his not having died in her mother's place) he didn't realize for many years.

Of course, he would always see something of Joanna in both her daughters, even Rachel, but not with the same intensity and in the same detail as he experienced casual associations. They were the children of Joanna, but a flight attendant, a dental hygienist, a Nobel laureate— these might for a moment actually be Joanna, causing a stab of loss so acute that it made him nauseous. To avoid the sensation, he slept only with women who looked nothing like his wife. Then he stopped sleeping with even these.

Joanna's imposters became fewer and fewer over the years, and he wondered if he was losing a working sense of her image. It had been a decade at least since anyone reminded him of her, and the absence of such Joannas in his life seemed suspicious to him now when the connections were besieging him like some relentless wartime shelling. He began to miss her again and, even while he dreaded other associations, to watch for her.

The only other face he actively courted was Rachel's, and it was with him every day from 2:30 to 3:30 in the afternoon, when the dayroom television was tuned to the staff's favorite soap opera. There on the screen was another Rachel, one of the regular characters, constantly embroiled in one or another silly plot of entanglement. He never followed the story, but he never failed to catch the show, even at the risk of appearing cute or eccentric to the staff. He didn't know the actress's name, and he tuned out her voice so that he could watch in her place his own daughter, tinted, tanned and embodied in a much more conventionally attractive person.

Then one day, in spite of his precautions, a particularly vivid association made itself felt.

He had forgotten to expect Sheila that afternoon, and he had been sampling the classical historians, having arranged the books he intended to visit in piles on the small circular table which stood at his strip of kitchenette. He had lost himself in Thucydides, pausing for a long time on the Athenians' nighttime invasion of Pylos. The stealth of it reminded him of something, the way all real tragedy crept up on you. The door buzzer snapped him out of it.

He was reluctant to leave Thucydides for the company of Sheila's disapproval. He looked at the table sadly—that would be her first complaint. She was always after him to "weed out" his books, as though unwelcome and dangerous ones had grown in among the flowers of his reading because he was a lazy gardener. But there was no time to return the books to the closet now: Sheila had crept up on him like the Athenian ships. The buzzer sounded again.

He opened the door to face a young man from the video rental store that had a delivery arrangement with the Estates. The shock of recognition left him speechless. At first he thought the boy reminded him of an actor he had seen play Achilles, in *Iphigenia*, say. But no, it was clear he had the face of Achilles himself, but pale, much paler than in life—it was the face of Achilles when Odysseus spoke with him in the Underworld. Meyer stepped back.

"You want to order videos?"

Meyer just stared. Then he became aware of others of the dead behind Achilles, reaching out their arms with longing for the blood that would make them lucid. And among them, but silent, intensely still and barely distinguishable, he recognized Joanna. He gasped.

"Sir! Mister? You all right? I'll get somebody—"

Meyer passed a hand over his eyes.

"Dad? Dad!"

Joanna was gone. Achilles was gone. In their place was Rachel—no, Sheila. She had looked like Rachel just then, for a moment.

Sheila took his arm and sat him down at the table. She pulled the other chair next to him and put her hand on his arm. "Dad? What is it? You scared that boy to death!"

He looked at her blankly. "The video store guy. He's gone . . . I told him you don't have a television—that *really* scared him." She snorted, but he had already heard the fear in her voice. He put his hand on hers.

"Okay." His voice was hoarse. "I'm okay."

Just then fat Christy, sent for by Achilles, bustled in chattering officiously and took his blood pressure and temperature. He sat limply, unresisting, until she was done.

"Pressure's a little high. But no temp. Not an event, I would say. I'll check him again in an hour."

Sheila was unusually subdued, so Christy turned to Meyer, raising her voice and speaking in deliberate syllables. "That all right with you, isn't it, Meyer? I'll be back in an hour." She spoke again to Sheila, this time in a stage whisper, as though he wouldn't be able to hear her from the other planet that his mind inhabited. "I don't think he needs to see anyone. I'll keep an eye on him, though. You staying a while?"

Sheila shut the door behind the aide. Meyer thought she brushed her eyes before turning to him.

"I'm okay, Sheila."

"I'll call the office and tell them I'm out for the rest of the afternoon. We can have some time that way."

He tried to protest. He didn't want her there now. But there was something fragile in the face he had long thought held no surprises for him, a trembling in the corners of her frown. The fact that she was living fifteen minutes from the Estates and that Rachel, his beloved Rachel, had moved away from their town years and years before to Portland to marry that man that hurt her occurred to him for the first time as significant.

The buzzer sounded again. It was a member of the cafeteria staff, the one who looked like George Eliot and the checker at the Safeway.

"Oh, Meyer. I forgot you were expecting company. We were worried about you. It's almost 2:30."

Sheila must have wondered about the soap opera, though the staff would already have told her, as they told her everything he did. But she sat by his side without comment during the program, sharing with him the milky-green vinyl-cushioned loveseat, lost in some thought that did not leave the same expression on her face as did her habitual caustic observation of his life. When the other Rachel appeared on the screen, he could feel her shift in her seat. He wondered if she saw it, the resemblance. If it hurt her to think that he needed his other daughter so much. He put his hand on her arm.

When the program was over, they rose together and started toward the hall. Sheila stopped abruptly and turned back to the glowing screen, where a businessman at an airport was impatiently checking his watch.

"Dad, doesn't he—"

The commercial ended, and another one advertising upcoming programs came onto the screen.

He looked at his daughter. She colored.

"It's just that for a moment, he looked like someone I know."

Walking down the hall with his older daughter, Meyer suddenly felt very tired and was surprised to find that he had been leaning heavily on her arm. He didn't think he'd be getting out to the college so much from now on. Or reading as much history. It took too much involvement.

He liked movies, though. Maybe he would get a television and sign up for videos. And he would let them come to him, the associations. It was too hard to fight them anymore.

"This was nice. I like having you come to see me."

The next time he would tell her—about Rachel in the program. About the resemblances—all of them. A little at first, though, so she could get used to it again.

"You don't have to stay. Christy will be back to check on me. And I think I'll take a little nap now."

She thought about it, looked at him closely, frowned. "I'll come Sunday. Take you out for brunch."

"Sunday. I'll look forward to it."

"Don't forget and then go and eat breakfast."

Sheila kissed him and left him at the door to his room.

He knew where this was going—at least, he thought so after seeing Joanna. And he didn't mind really. It had been so good to see Joanna again.

He lifted the blind and looked out on the courtyard. It was raining, as usual, and the benches looked bleak and deserted now, but in less than a month, the sun would reappear and the residents would start to drift outside. He would join them, telling them they all looked like someone much younger from this life or before. They wouldn't mind. He would take Sadie's arm and walk with her or find a bench where they could sit together.

For now, he found he liked the rain, now that he knew where it fell—on Sheila driving her minivan home past fields of wet but stalwart little leaguers and on Rachel reading by the window in her Portland flat; on Christy checking medicine charts, ignorant of those who had shared her moon-shaped face—on them, too; on Dutchy the last time Meyer saw him smile and on Joanna who had made him smile; on kingdom past and kingdom come; on, as the writer said, all the living and the dead. How could he have been so blind?

SAFE SHALL BE MY GOING

Prologue

(*West Midlands, 1948*)

The same shameful trouble, it was, the same secret, away up in Northumberland.

It had been queer enough, Kate chancing on Agnes Pearce like that, when there were over a hundred women entered in the county home foods competitions that Saturday in August (a bold number as the shortages made it an adventure to do the baking and preserve-making), twenty in the red-currant jam alone. It seemed like fate, destined-like, thought Kate, flushed with foreboding, that out of all of them she'd come upon her husband Tom's old sergeant's missus in the relishes and condiments, especially as Agnes was only entering the one judging (chutney) and was only just back from India after the 1947 handing-over. It was strange, then, meeting Agnes, and it was stranger still they had the same secret. Kate couldn't eat her tea for thinking on it.

How was it, Kate had wondered in the thirty years since the War, the Platoon wives managed to miss each other, when the Platoon itself had got such notice, coming out as it did, almost intact? Intact, that is, except a few early lads and, of course, their lieutenant, and with commendations, too—which they would've won, wouldn't they, surviving so long, unless they'd been outright cowards and hid out for the duration, and anyone knowing her Tom would know right away he wouldn't've stood for that, for shirking. They'd got lots of notice after the war, as there were so few men coming home, and this a whole Platoon entire, almost. How they missed each other for so long, she'd wondered—out loud, too, at times, but Tom always said he didn't like thinking about it, the War, so she dropped it.

Until the home foods, that is, and meeting Agnes Pearce, whose husband, it turned out, when she and Agnes hit it off, was sergeant in Tom's company and at the same time as Tom, and at Valenciennes at the end. He was one of them, that Platoon that nobody could figure out how they all survived, that seemed charmed someone once said in the newspaper. But that wasn't all, wasn't in fact the point, the thing that fate planned for them, the reason, she thought, that she found Agnes Pearce there amongst all the other women at the competitions. It was that her man, too, Agnes's, had a secret, and—so the two of them reckoned once they compared some points—the same secret, in a house in Northumberland, on the sea.

Kate sat with Agnes for a while in the tea tent, a hot wind blowing in dust, and watched the committee ladies spread handkerchiefs over the cakes. What she was thinking was whether Agnes was thinking the same as herself, though she couldn't have said exactly what it was she was thinking, it was that peculiar, their having the same trouble. It was only now she shared it with someone that she could think of it as a trouble. It was like doubling the oddness she always felt when she thought of the Platoon. And when she did think of it—the Platoon—at that moment, then she and Agnes came to it *together* (on instinct mostly) because there was something about them all coming out intact—well nearly all, except that blessed lieutenant, who was somehow responsible, so they twigged, by heroics, or sweet nature, or discipline (how would they know, since their men wouldn't talk about it?) for them all coming out of it, excepting himself. They came to the idea that they should look up the rest, the ones who had been green girls at the time or young mams, some of them, several of them not yet Platoon wives nor sweethearts at first, only meeting their men for the first time after the war. They should look them all up, to see if they, too, like Kate and Agnes, lost their men annually so it seemed, and sometimes in between, to the secret in Northumberland. And when a long while later they discovered it to be so amongst all of the wives (allowing for the dead and the one they never ran to ground), when they found that it belonged to every living man in that magic Platoon of theirs, they called that secret The Platoon's Whore.

Part I

Chapter 1

Far, far from Wipers I long to be.
Where German snipers can't get at me.
Dark is my dugout, cold are my feet.
Waiting for Whizzbangs to send me to sleep.

—Trench Song, WWI

(*France, 1916*)

Sergeant Colin Pearce was at his wits' end with the men. He knew now from a glut of experience that death could smell weakness of any kind, be it fear or exhaustion or simple lack of attention, and he was at his wits' end with struggling to overcome this platoon's weakness—that was Disorder. Not that the men weren't well trained (they were mostly Old Sweats, not conscripts and not inexperienced) or were sloppy or lazy or stupid (though there were the ignorant ones). They just could not fix with one another; there was none of that esprit de corps ("esprit de *corpse*" others joked, but not this lot, they weren't up to it), that chumminess you expect, even amongst a few. There were no friends even. It wasn't that they were unpleasant men; they were coarse, like any lads, but they were as kind and thoughtful as you could expect them to be in this place. And they were ordinary brave. But they were a rag-and-tail group—he put it up to that, that they were the remains like, of other companies that were all but obliterated.

Mabb was typical of them in many ways. He'd joined up with pals at the beginning of the war and was in field hospital with rheumatic fever when the 2nd Middlesex went over into the mist at Neuve Chapelle in '15. Between bouts of delirium, he asked after his chums. There were no wounded returning, he was told, the advance must have been a stunning success. By the time he was shipped home with a bad heart, the truth, as much as his health, had released him from his battalion: three companies of the 2nd Middlesex almost to a man lay dead, mown down in rows by the Jaeger machine gunners. With them went his entire platoon and the pals he knew for brothers. After the Somme, the clamor for men at the Western Front all but drowned out Mabb's heart murmur, so that no army doctor could claim to hear it, and no one objected when he asked to be sent back. He requested a new posting, with lads he didn't know. And that's how he found himself in the summer of 1916 with Sergeant Pearce's platoon.

They were all survivors like Mabb—of Neuve Chapelle and the Marne, the first and second Ypres. Pulled together like some general's grim joke, a company of the undead, they met here together, but separate, individuals, and though there was the odd gesture at sharing, joking, song even, it never took. And though they went over the top as one and with the loose confidence of experience, they lost sight of each other, neglected to cover, came back to find one or another of them missing. And casualties were high; they were always high like this when there was none of that esprit and no one was looking out for a particular chum. He was at his wits' end with it.

Another in a long line of subalterns was killed, along with Mr. Hawken and Mr. Phillipson, and then they were relieved by a company of Royal Scots infantry. It made the sergeant uneasy to have to wait for a superior to be assigned to his fractured group of men. Not that Second Lieutenant Smelton had pulled them together. He didn't have the broader view, the vision of his platoon as a whole. He looked closely at maps, as was proper, sent out his watch to be synchronized, gave orders that made sense to Sergeant Pearce and ground his teeth with frustration when they couldn't pull it off. And then he was gone, blown to pieces, nothing left but ends and raw bits. But at least Mr. Smelton had been there to share in the losses, to make them his instead of the sergeant's, and the sergeant couldn't help but wish that the promised replacement would arrive before they were sent up again. Otherwise, they would answer to Major Perrine with the other platoons, and that, Pearce knew, would mean he was on his own.

An officer did arrive, another new lieutenant, another young toff, but sweeter this time than any they'd had so far. The men took to him immediately, and while the sergeant watched with an eye sharpened in experience, he thought he saw his men fuse, oozing together like damp clots, waking up to one another under the nurturing attention of their young commander. By the end of the first week in reserve, the lieutenant knew all of their names, and somehow—not by asking directly—had got out of them their counties and girls and whether they were married with kiddies and all. Suddenly these sulky lads had things to complain of hopefully or to show the lieutenant. (Dixon revealed something of himself when he requested a needle for picking out a splinter while pus oozed and bubbled from the gash over his left ear; and young Gaddes had a photograph of his dogs, but not his girl.) He had soothed and comforted and, yes, dressed them down—a good thing, that, or he'd be too soft—and was accepted as the center of their world, their heart and mind, and the sergeant could relax again, he thought, and be something less vital than a heart or a mind. The arm, he thought now, the right arm of their leader.

They were sent in again after too short a rest in squalid French billets, and the sergeant could feel a tremor of portent in the regimental's orders for a night raid. So he was not surprised when shelling forced his raiders to retire before they'd even breached the wire. They made the fire trench short one man and carrying with them a grim report, which he passed on to the lieutenant.

"Sampson's still out there, Lieutenant. Skinner tried to pull him back, but his foot's caught in a Lewis-gun cart. Skinner and Evans want to go back for him."

The lieutenant lowered his eyes for a moment. He had lashes like a girl's, and these gave him a doe-like look, his delicate head poised on its stem of long white neck. As always, his voice was calm and soft as salve. "Have them go, then, Sergeant; they'll get an idea what we need to cut him out. If he's bleeding elsewhere, or he makes too much noise, we'll have to take the foot off quickly."

Pearce shot the men a look—Evans could be useless, windy under heavy fire, though he tried not to show it.

But Skinner . . .

"Yes, sir. Skinner! . . . Evans! . . . out you go . . . before next flare."

Skinner and Evans found that Sampson's foot was wedged tight under the abandoned cart, and there was a hole the size of pippin in his chest. He was pale and babbling, and the Germans must have reckoned exactly where they were by now. There was nothing for it, and Skinner's face ran with tears as he chopped hurriedly above the ankle with the hand-axe the sergeant had slipped to him in the moment before he climbed over. Sampson reared back and looked at the crying man in horror. He began to scream in earnest. Evans was sick beside the two of them. A light-shell rocket went up, and in the sudden midday glare it cast as it swayed back and forth, the three white faces froze with fear. At the moment the flare died, a bomb burst. Only Evans came back, with shrapnel along one side of his body and vomit all down his front.

After such outings as these the mood deepened. Sergeant Pearce watched his lieutenant tensely. Did the man realize? He watched him calmly give the order, lead the rush, pull them back, visit their dugouts, peer with interest at their photographs, squeeze their shoulders, run a hand through the young ones' hair. At least they hadn't lost that many since he came. Only Sampson and Skinner, so far, though they'd had to send Evans back to Blighty with his wounds. Still, Pearce sensed the lieutenant's unease, though he moved with quiet grace through the line and smiled warmly, easily. He got a lot of letters.

Chapter 2

A leaping wind from England,
The skies without a stain,
Clean cut against the morning
Slim poplars after rain,
The foolish noise of sparrows
And starlings in a wood -
After the grime of battle
We know that these are good.

—from "Back to Rest"
by William Noel Hodgson

(Yorkshire, 1915)

My dearest Richard,

Moggie says to tell you "pack us a few rats, there's a good lad," as the stories we hear of the front all involve rats in some form or another, and you know she's never so sleek and satisfied with herself as when she has had rat en croute. I was witness last Thursday to those awful Atkinson boys telling their little sister Delia that the men *at the front are often forced to <u>eat</u> rat. It had our Moggie in a green slough of envy. The cat deserves a proper name, I think. If I hear Mrs. Lanton refer to her even once more as "Pussums," I shall have to do something violent to the woman. How does one name things? I think of this all the time. For instance, how did Hutton-Le-Hole get its name? Or Dool-'a-Swalebeck? I shall have to ask Alphaeus; he seems to know the answers to things like this. Dales history is his forte, I suppose. The writing vicar? The vicarious author? Vicious pennings? Say these things aloud; that's always best with a letter— and poetry, of course.*

I love writing to you. Except that I pause at each sentence expecting to hear you respond. (You are such a <u>good</u> listener. Is that a good thing in an officer?) I do love writing you, but I detest posting the letters. Curious Mrs. Sturgess keeps her post office in the shop with as much fervor as a hanging judge, I think. Since last I described a visit there, she has managed to attract a number of the local semi-employed to the spot shortly before pick-up times to witness the flurry of postings that inevitably takes place just before the boy arrives with his satchel. Can you imagine that lazy hostler Ruddock and his boy, and Willem Sadler the odd-jobsman, and several older male habitués of the village streets, lounging around the counter in anticipation of the mail? As a result, now I not only have to undergo a thorough catechizing from Herself, but my answers are discussed and commented on by all the onlookers. It is most mortifying. Fortunately, the last time I was there (it was that time that I was inspired to send <u>two</u> letters in one day, and this the second, for the evening post), Phyllis Whitehead was posting, as well. It was obvious to me that she had not expected to encounter such a large assembly. The novelty of my own appearance having grown a bit tarnished with these gentlemen, and Douglas Whitehead having only just left for France again in the last few weeks since his recovery, they turned their attention to poor Phyllis. The opening knell is always sounded by the postmistress herself.

"Mrs. Whitehead, and would that be a letter for the Captain at the front?"

"Yes, Mrs. Sturgess, it is, as you can see by the address."

"You were careful not to include anything that could be interpreted to the enemy's advantage, weren't you, should it fall into the wrong hands, I mean?"

(dryly) "I tried to restrain myself from giving the particulars of military maneuvers, yes, Mrs. Sturgess." (here I felt a new respect for P. Whitehead, whose chilly Glorious Empire reserve had always seemed a bit off-putting before)

(up pops old Martin Conlon from the nap into which he had slipped as he leant against the haberdashery case, with an aspect of what one could only describe as ironic interest)

"Thee wants to send cheerin' news, Mrs. W., is what thee wants. Send 'im sum of tha' then, did thee?"

"Very cheering, Mr. Conlon. Very cheering."

(postmistress peering curiously at envelope and weighing it in her hand thoughtfully) "About the harvest, dear? There's not much that's cheering about the harvest, I think, this year—"

"No, I did not discuss the harvest, Mrs. Sturgess. Nor the shortages, nor blackouts. Will that do?"

(hostler here) "Well, I don' mean t' imply summat, Missus, but what else is there t'write on, save 'arvest or *shortages or blackouts, as there be a war on?"*

(Phyllis sending one a look of exasperation) "Would you like me to open it for you so that you might examine the contents and approve it?"

(stirrings and rumblings here, "tut-tuts" and "no need ters")

(postmistress bridling) "The Censors will be doing that, of course, dear . . . why, you don't want to put in anything compromising, you know . . . personal like . . ."

(all of the men leaning forward now to catch every word)

". . . connubial, say, or . . . private."

(Phyllis red and swelling) "I beg your pardon?"

(Conlon, with exaggerated patience) "Of a personal natur', Mrs. W, like Ellie Bastow did last Thursday, in her sweet'art's letter. Oh, I bet tha' made them Censors blush, too, din't?"

(murmurs of "it did tha' ")

"And how—?"

(postmistress) "We could not persuade her to alter it as she said it had taken her all the half-holiday to write it in the first place."

(hostler) "But tha' bit about 'im in 'is uniform and all . . ."

(Conlon) "Steamy, I think they calls it."

"I don't see—"

Having slipped my own letter into Mrs. Sturgess's receiving box, I pull Phyllis, who is rising like a large loaf, from the shop before blood is drawn. Several of Mrs. Lanton's miraculous rock cakes and cuppers later, she is soothed, I having assured her that only letters from the front are censored, and that, even then, the officers' letters are not, or, at least, are self-censored, which amounts to the same thing. Is this not so? She left replete with rock cake and left me replete with the very details of the letter the postmistress's gang had been trying so hard to pry from her. I feel like Moggie with a rat.

I asked Phyllis what she thought we should name our Moggie, and she suggested Raffles, after the character in Middlemarch because (and this was painful to hear) she has always considered our Moggie a pushing and vulgar cat! I was greatly offended, though she has a point.

I only really feel alive now when I am writing you. I take my famous walk every afternoon, and these autumn days, the air turns that lovely crisp prickly feeling, and the leaves on the drives are like silvered blossoms, and voices can be heard from Uttleys' in the evening calling the animals home. When one passes Marshalls', the warmth comes off the stables like a cloak to envelop one, and I know that Mrs. Lanton will be calculating ways to put by precious sugar and even butter for tarts, and that the odor of savory will waft soon from the kitchen. But it is all like paper stagecraft to me without you. Until I write it—then it bursts back at me with all the vitality that was missing when I experienced it. Do you understand? I have to share the world with you, and this is how I shall do it, every day. I only hope you receive them all, my letters, and one a day, as they are written, though I know it is unreasonable to suppose so.

Good-bye for now, my love, my perfect love. (Take that, you Censors!)

Your Emma

Chapter 3

'tis an unweeded garden
That grows to seed; things rank and gross in nature
Possess it merely.
—*Hamlet*, I, ii

(*France, 1916*)

It went against all his sergeant's instincts when the lieutenant read the first letter out to the men. The first he read to them, that is, for he was drowning in letters before then; she must do nothing at all but write it seemed. When the mail carts couldn't get through to the front line, it meant a fat packet of letters waiting for him in reserve. It was a joke with the quartermaster-sergeant and the post-corporal. But not with the men. They watched him hungrily, resentful of his attention and of the letters.

It could have turned bad, but the night Skinner and Sampson caught the shell was a terrible night for all of them. They'd had to go back out right away: Jerry was thinning out and backing off. Orders always followed this kind of lull: take the next trench and the next. Push, the push is on. Little Nevin Benton had the heaves as usual just before they went over, and of course he was the one to find Sampson's foot, still wedged where it had been left in the gun-cart, but without the rest of Sampson, the white shard of bone gleaming in the light of a German flare. The sergeant had crawled around to him to push his mouth hard to keep him from screaming and taking a Jerry stick bomb or pineapple, and to hold closed his eyes that wanted to stare at Sampson's foot. When he was able to drag the boy into the next trench, no more than a gully with its sides blown in and the dugouts smashed, where bodies from both sides had been piled for a parados, several lads crawled over to help quieten him. There was something in the boy's face that made him think they were for it now—too bloody weary to try anymore. Too sick.

Then the shelling stopped and the lieutenant took out his letter. Damn the man! Couldn't he see they needed him now? The sergeant tried to stand, but his legs gave out. He couldn't even raise a hand to signal his officer. The lieutenant's voice drifted over to where Pearce had collapsed, his head against a bloated corpse (and he didn't care a bit, he was that fagged).

" '. . . as the cows aren't giving milk, says Dairyman Uttley, insisting they can sense the airship bombings. Evidently, one can pull a squirt or two if it's only a London raid, a mere trickle if Yarmouth, and of course, the beasts go dry when the bombs reach Leeds. The Sturgess maintains, however, that he's got a black market going and there's milk for those who are willing to pay. All I know for certain is that Mrs. L served us "blancmange" made with gelatin entirely, and no milk, but with eggs! Can you imagine? She gave me no warning, and Alphaeus had come to dinner, along with a fat brother clergyman, the aptly named Mr. Plumpton, from

Scarborough, a school chum, I think, very ponderous girth, the kind of gentleman who measures and evaluates his days in meals. You cannot imagine the combination of gelatin, sugar, and egg—like something left when the dog has been sick. I saw his eyes goggle at the mess . . .' "

What in world was the man thinking? Had he gone to shock? It went against all the sergeant's instincts, that, their officer sharing his letters with Other Ranks.

But the silence in the trench made him look around. They were listening, listening with expressions of rapture. With hungry open mouths they listened, some of them, and some of them with their eyes closed, and some smiling. Boys that used Fuck and Bugger-All to make a point of everything they said, they looked . . . they looked *charmed* by the bloody thing.

" '. . . and Mrs. Lanton's "I did warn you, Missus," which wasn't true at all, but only spoken for their benefit, though I couldn't hold it against her, not with Mr. Plumpton turning <u>muck-all-green</u> . . .' " (almost hearty laugh here from some of the men; sniggering at least from everyone) " '. . . and Alphaeus apologizing as though he had made the pudding himself. The portly Plumpton bolted for the door. Alphaeus followed, removing both their hats from the stand. He, at least, turned to me to press my hand and say he didn't blame me, not in the least.' " (There was some chuckling at this, and then, with surprising vigor, shushing.)

"Shut yer gob, Everett! I can't 'ear the lieutenant over yer noises!"

"I'm afraid I can't read any louder."

"Ah, that's all right, sir. We can 'ear you sound enough."

"I'll finish, then, shall I?"

"Yes, sir. Is there mich more?" This was Benton's thin alto, brittle with eagerness.

"Not much, Nevin."

(There were a few groans of disappointment.)

" 'Alphaeus looked a little wild as he whispered about some confidence he'd wanted to share. Something he'd hoped to gain by Plumpton's visit. A preferment—something. I'm still unclear, but it has all the markings of a coup, with our mild Alphaeus in place as pretender. We made a hurried date to meet at the vicarage (he has promised me a coffee!) after matins tomorrow, though I had thought to miss early prayers this week and accompany Phyllis to the children's infirmary, where she rolls bandages with Lady Superintendent Mrs. Irene Belliston of the Red Cross. (Phyllis has visions of becoming a VAD of one kind or another.) But Alphaeus made it sound so much like intrigue that I shall have to forgo the infirmary. And you shall have to wait to hear until tomorrow, if your tomorrow corresponds with mine. Meanwhile, my—' " Here the lieutenant stopped abruptly and folded the letter.

"Is there more, sir?"

"She says good-bye and keep well."

"'Til nex' time, eh, sir?"

"Good-bye and keep well until next time, of course. You lads sleep now. We can do nothing more until the runner arrives with orders."

"'Night, sir."

"Goodnigh', Lieutenant. Expec' ya'll hear fre 'er soon as we're back in reserve, eh."

"I expect I will. Good-night."

They were kept alive on her letters, though it wasn't as if they never got their own—some of them got almost regular mail, including postcards and even parcels. (There was, for instance, Sergeant's Agnes, who, though never much for writing, sent jars of jams and pickled onions wrapped in grey woolen mufflers.) But *she* never sent parcels, no sweets or cakes, though she had a cook, that Mrs. Lanton, who was magic at conjuring ingredients, except milk, of course, since the raids had disturbed the cows. The lieutenant's wife never sent him parcels, but she wrote and she wrote, and the letters kept them all alive. Or, it could be said, they lived on anticipation and suspense. They wouldn't, not one of them, dare to die: they wanted to know what happened next. They wouldn't be left hanging like that, unfulfilled. It kept them sharp. It filled them with strength and wits and honed their sympathy for one another, synchronized their reflexes, so to speak, so that when a piece of shrapnel ratatatted against Bolton's helmet, Mallow's head sang, and when Craddock, intent on bayoneting a Jerry sniper, allowed three other Huns to creep up behind him, Mabb and Dixon, from opposite flanks and with their backs to the scene, spun and took the Germans before they got their mate. In fact, after the night of Sampson and Skinner, no one died, and wounds were not worth remarking on and certainly they were not blighties, not that any one of the men would have let himself be sent back home, even if he lost an arm or had a hole in his head the size of an orange. That was it, they all had holes in their heads, the sergeant, too, for wanting the letters so much, for fighting so well and surviving entire, just to get back to trench to hear the next one.

"'... as Leach the sexton told me yesterday. You were right about Leach, Richard—he's Uriah Heep to a T. I don't wonder Alphaeus doesn't see it, though, he's such a naïve soul. Don't you think it was naughty of God to give such a baby as our Alphaeus that cherubic face and those eyebrows like little peaked roofs that couldn't hide a pilfered lardy cake from the village idiot?

" 'Well, our Heep that is Leach came oiling around here yesterday just to report on the terrible hash Alphaeus made of his one great foray into church politics. Why he even dared to suggest a shift of the Riding choir to our little village is beyond me, except that that awful Plumpton—remember, he of the delicate gustatory sensibilities?—had got him so excited at the prospect, and Plumpton probably knew Alphaeus well enough to know that his one weakness is for music, sacred of course, but low tunes, too, as you and I know. Have you heard him whistle Alexander's Ragtime Band? It is a revelation, not altogether holy. Not that he would think of directing the choir to sing anything but hymns and carols. It's just that a man who whistles Alexander's Ragtime Band, well, he has more depths to his soul than at first may strike the eye, and of course, the deeper the man, the greater a field of prospect for the devil, not to mention the greater the abyss into which he may fall. Or so I am informed by that student of human nature, Leach, whose obvious relish over Alphaeus's reprimand by the bishop made my hackles rise.

" 'Oh, you must pass on a little bit of related information to Mr. Bobbet—' "

"Wha', is it me, then, Lieutenant?"

"Yes, Bobbet, my wife remembers something you had me ask her in one of my letters . . . hum . . . here it is: 'He must be quite clever at understanding men, your Mr. Bobbet, for he is right—Plumpton was only using Alphaeus for another purpose.' There you go, Bobbet."

A few men around Bobbet gave him a congratulatory punch. He beamed.

" '. . . for another purpose entirely. It was to bring to the attention of the Bishop at Ripon that the present Riding choir, based in Kyedale under the management of Vicar Ramsey, had been for some time engaged in the interesting practice of performing penny concerts (with cakes and tea) throughout the dales. . . .' " ("Oh, ho!'s" from those who caught on, or pretended to, right away)

" ' . . . Worse still, not all the music they performed could be called sacred, and suspiciously, the Kyedale church chancel was just given a quite new face in polish, and the clergy chairs are now sporting cushions! I doubt that our friend Plumpton ever intended to back Alphaeus at all. It appears Plumpton has had a long-standing and widely acknowledged rivalry with Ramsey for years, and pretending to argue on Alphaeus's behalf, he took the opportunity of our own dear vicar's bid for the shire choir to expose the matter of the Riding choir concert enterprise and the rewards thereof. And poor Alphaeus! He never meant to suggest that Ramsey did not deserve a shire choir, but only that he, Alphaeus, did. Well, the whole thing was a terrible embarrassment, or so Leach reports. But I think that Alphaeus came off all right. It really must be apparent to others as well as ourselves what a sweet and guileless dupe he is in the hands of dishonorable men, don't you agree? I hope so. In any case, he has written the most harrowing mea culpa to Ramsey, of whom I know nothing except this concert scheme, but who I am sure deserves neither abjection nor esteem from our beautiful-souled Alphaeus.' "

"Innit just like people, then, ter do a man that way?" It was Bobbet, exercising his recently acknowledged understanding of human nature.

"That's plain, that is, Bobb*eee*," commented Craddock, along with other men. "But what I want to know is did this Leach feller put in his kit wi' that fat clergyman friend of our vicar's, eh?"

"That's an interesting question, Craddock." The lieutenant looked thoughtful. "I'll ask my wife what she thinks of it in my next letter. Meanwhile, I have another message here . . ." There were stirrings of interest among the men. "It's for Worrall. She says she'll send a copy of *David Copperfield* along for you if you like. She was quite gratified by your interest in *Middlemarch* after the one letter, and she hopes you're enjoying it."

"Tell 'er, if you would, that is, Lieutenant, that it's hard going, but it's right up ter mark. Only, I dun' believe it could be by a woman, sir. It's too straight, d'yer know?"

The lieutenant laughed. "She'll appreciate the point. Meanwhile, would you like the Dickens—*David Copperfield*, I mean? It's the book in which Uriah Heep appears."

"The man that's makin' poor vicar's life a misery?"

"Yes, that's the man."

"Yeh, I'd like that 'un, too. Only I can't promise ter start it right away. I'm dead set on finishin' this 'un, first."

"I'll be sure to warn her."

"Any more messages, Lieutenant?" The sergeant felt he should ask what was in all their minds.

"Not in this one, Sergeant, but I'm sure my wife would be happy to answer any man's questions and very happy to hear his remarks, if any of you would pass them on."

In this way, they started receiving their own brief messages from the lieutenant's wife. For some were interested in one thing, some in another. Bradshaw wanted to know about the effects of the coastal shelling on the whole countryside. Did the chickens stop laying, too? His father had a farm in the south downs, and he thought perhaps the bombs might be felt there as well. McMichael the rake was always after the girls' stories—domestics and farmers' and merchants' daughters, and the tearoom waitresses, wherever they popped up in one or another narrative. The only ones he didn't ask after were a pair of munitions workers down from Edinburgh, visiting their auntie, though whether it was because he thought the work unfeminine or because he did not like to be reminded of the war, no one knew. Like the would-be lover he was, he followed each of the other girls' trails into another plot and another, following some even after their hasty marriages to soldiers like himself, to the loss of their men and their breakdowns or remarriages, and so on. Bolton had a fondness for Mrs. Lanton's kitchen creations, although they were reported as increasingly unpalatable as the war progressed and the good woman's ingenuity was stretched to its limit. Some of the lads had bets on that Bolton was in love with Mrs. Lanton; others thought he fancied himself becoming a cook after the war. Craddock joked that what he really loved was horror stories, and there was nothing could be thought more horrible than some of Mrs. Lanton's cooking.

There was always a part of each letter which the lieutenant kept to himself. Most of the men would be nursing their own thoughts, following the individual plot of their fancy, and they wouldn't notice their officer's own blank sadness and longing. The sergeant sometimes slid over to the man and gently encouraged him.

"She all right then, your missus? Keeping spirits up and all, sir?"

"Yes, yes, she just says she misses me, Sergeant. That's all that's left."

"You'll be home, sir. War won't go on forever."

The lieutenant looked at him in surprise. A snort of laughter burst from him, making a repellent contrast to the man's beauty. "That's a most unrealistic observation, especially coming from a realist like you, Pearce."

The sergeant was momentarily covered in confusion. "I just meant . . . I mean to say—"

"No, no, you're right, Pearce. It can't go on forever. We'll all be dead eventually, and there will be no more war then, eh?" He snorted again, then patted the sergeant on the back. "Never mind. I'm a bastard to suggest it, eh? Look at us. Best fighting platoon on the . . . on the Western Front. We'll get them all back, won't we?"

"Yes, sir, I think we will."

"Of course. We will."

"Yes, Lieutenant."

"All back."

"Yes, Lieutenant, we will. Yes, we will."

Chapter 4

She'll get them all back, the sergeant thought, but didn't say so. He just watched, watched the men throw themselves into the fighting with a desperation so palpable it was like a caul of protection over them. He wouldn't swear that the bullets bounced off it, or that the shrapnel skidded and whined along its edge, but he, too, felt almost invulnerable, with a preternatural awareness of every tiny moment as it ricocheted off the next and the next. Nothing happened too quickly for his judgment to take effect. And it was not for the men, he was ashamed to realize, that he suddenly had the lightning capabilities he needed to survive—it was for the letters, her letters, which in their way had made enough sense, just enough sense out of the madness that had overwhelmed him on the night that Sampson and Skinner died, just enough to make it worth returning to trench again, once more. To find out what happened. What was going to happen, to the vicar Alphaeus, the housekeeper Mrs. Lanton, the fields and the cows, the cat and the postmistress? Were they real? Did they exist and would they exist when the platoon—some of it—made it back? It didn't matter; it kept him going. As long as there was something left to resolve itself, as long as the plot never played out, but promised, like the cinema adventures, to continue . . . to be continued . . .

Worrall was the first to get his own letter. It came, actually, with the *David Copperfield.* Worrall opened and folded and opened and folded it again every few minutes, gazing at it like it was a holy relic. He wore it in his breast pocket by his heart. When the order to advance came, he took the Dickens with him, but wrote out a painstaking recommendation for the *Middlemarch* and slipped it between the pages for the lads in the next line following them to find. No one asked to see Worrall's letter, and the lieutenant had seemed unaware of its existence as he passed the bundle of platoon letters to Pearce and Bolton for distributing. It left the sergeant wondering a little, but he kept his thoughts to himself and watched Worrall, along with the others, continue an enchanted dance through the wasted landscape, immune to disaster.

With the kind of irony this war seemed to enjoy, once they got the reputation that comes with outrageous triumphs of self-preservation ("Well, lads, we'll make the Fritzie Blacklist yet!"), they found themselves called forward much more often than other platoons, dragging in their wake the rest of their own company, who were confused and resentful of this notoriety and, unlike Pearce's mob, were continually depleted by losses. But the platoon's ferocity only increased with each show, fueled by desire for the letters. They might be sitting fat with promise back at headquarters. Or they might have been brought forward instead by awestruck runners who were given the unconventional direct order by an amused major or colonel, during even the most savage clash, to deliver—posthaste!—these particular mailbags to trench.

Worrall did not answer his letter, as far as the sergeant could tell, but he got another a few days later in the lieutenant's wife's hand, which they all knew as well now as their own. He didn't seem surprised or excited, but strangely peaceful when it arrived, and when he had read it, he folded it carefully and pocketed it with the other.

A week later, Bolton's letter came, and a few days after that, Dixon's. By the time they reached Chambrai, every man had received a letter from the lieutenant's wife, and several more than one. Every man but the sergeant, that is. For every man but the sergeant had asked for his own plot, had relayed through the lieutenant an interest in some thing, some story within her daily life that was following its own meandering track, veering away from the story she shared with her husband and which he continued to read for them every time the letters arrived, the story which never ended except with a promise for more, a hint of an ending and never an end.

The sergeant burned to ask her. He burned to have the runner hand him the packet only to find the letter on top, the fattest one, addressed to him, in that hand. There were always smudges on the letters, as though she couldn't keep the ink off her fingers, as though she caressed the letters with inky fingers when she was done, as though caressing them himself (as he did when he passed them on, to Worrall and Dixon and the others) he could touch those fingertips beneath their prints, rising up from the contents of the letters cool and fresh to press themselves on his own hot, feverish fingers.

But he couldn't bring himself to do it, to send a query along with the lieutenant's letter. For one thing, he couldn't think of a question to ask, a particular story to ask after . . . but that wasn't the only reason. He was afraid of her answer, afraid of condescension, of a sense of detachment. He couldn't bear to have words directed to himself from her that were any less personal than the ones at the end of the lieutenant's letters, the ones the lieutenant kept from them, words that he knew must be warm with intimacy, sensual with secret empathy. Of course, he hadn't read any of the men's letters, so he couldn't know how much of herself she withheld from them, how much she wrapped in coolness. But he was taking no chances: he could not have endured something chatty and benign while the thought of the lieutenant's letters continued to make him burn.

And . . . he didn't have a question. Or rather, the question he had—it was not a question, really, it was a declaration, an avowal—was one he couldn't ask, couldn't write. It was a way of purging the heat from his fingertips.

What he did know—they all did—was that the stories never ended. The sergeant couldn't have said when it first occurred to him, or when it first took shape in all of their minds as a conviction, that the stories *could* never end, that the end of a story would mean the end of will. The magic would evaporate, leaving them exposed and helpless. So without reading them, he knew that the men's stories continued, that McMichael's girls might marry, but their lives would continue to contain promises that would evoke interest in the lieutenant's wife, who passed that interest on to McMichael and armed him against death; that Mrs. Lanton would forever pursue the perfect pudding, in spite of shortages of sugar and milk, and that her travails would continue to engage Bolton forever and lend him a shield against the Hun; that nothing would ever be resolved, but would spin its history out unconcluded, as long as the war lacked resolution.

Only the sergeant noticed when the lieutenant stopped reading his letters aloud. By then the men were receiving them regularly. Only the sergeant, who got none of his own, wondered how she managed to write them all, to write, every week or so, a letter, be it a short one, to each man in a platoon of twenty-three men (all that were left of the forty-eight original lads, and a sight more than many British platoons could still boast). And there was the paper to think of. (Agnes, short on words, but long on thrift, had resorted to the paper off the butcher's meat until he wrote to tell her he could smell blood on it, though that was a lie: it was only the thought of it as made him gag.) And postage, though letters to the lads only cost a penny apiece, probably not a sacrifice for a lady of her class. But the sergeant thought of these things, only he did, and only he noticed the dwindling of the lieutenant's readings, in spite of the lieutenant's letters continuing to arrive at the old rate. And it was the sergeant alone who noticed, and kept to himself, the change in the lieutenant.

The outburst, as he thought of it, was the first hint, that momentary lapse in the lieutenant's characteristic self-possession when he had snorted twice and patted the sergeant on the back. That one glimpse of the young man's buried pessimism marked the sergeant's first awareness of the lieutenant's unraveling. Then there was the falling off of the readings, which never appeared to trouble the men, well-supplied as they were with their own letters. It was only the sergeant—letter-less but for the hasty notes he found in Agnes's parcels—it was the sergeant, burning for a letter from the lieutenant's wife but getting none, who could see that the lieutenant hoarded his messages now, shared them infrequently and with little attention to their order. The plot was hard to follow now he skipped some. It would have irritated the sergeant, who lived for these letters, if he hadn't known it was evidence of something worse going on in the lieutenant, their beloved lieutenant, and so something worse for themselves.

One time he was startled to hear the lieutenant read about . . .

" ' . . . Stonecroft's whiskey . . .' "

The sergeant could remember nothing about Stonecroft or his whiskey in a previous letter.

" ' . . . with which the woman had cleaned the wound. Well, you can imagine the row that ensued, in spite of the great wide crack running from behind his left ear to his forehead. I think he would have preferred a plaster of dung, as did the wild Celts—do I have that right? Or is it ancient Egyptians?—to her wasting good liquor like that on doctoring him. I don't know where he had found her, this woman, but she could swear like a sailor . . .' "

Despite his confusion, the sergeant lost himself in it, this easy flow of her life, renewing his strength, his will.

" ' . . . made me look away, as though the scene were too squalid for my tender sensibilities. Really, it's Alphaeus himself who nearly fainted . . .' "

The vicar was the sergeant's favorite character, though he couldn't have said why; he'd little tolerance for such weak, sappy men back home. But now the clergyman, though hundreds of miles away, comforted Pearce, as he could never have comforted his own stout country flock.

" ' . . . had to smile at Alphaeus's outrage—to think, an aging blackguard of an artist like Stonecroft inviting us both for tea, and then forgetting the invitation and carrying on with his latest model of sorts in that manner, brawling and getting himself thrashed by her (she's built like a navy ship), and it turns out that that cherished bottle of whiskey was not only a vessel of curative, but the original weapon which had come to hand.' "

This letter, like all the others, had a story that promised to carry on for some time, though the introduction of the painter Stonecroft and his adventures must have been contained in one of the letters the lieutenant had failed to share with them. The sergeant turned over in his mind the image of Stonecroft's whiskey, wondering where it would surface again, under what circumstances it might make an encore. Other such talismans, like Mrs. Lanton's custards and the lieutenant's wife's daily walks to post her letters, recurred like signposts to signal the routes the plot would take. They contributed to the platoon's familiarity with the encapsulated world of the lieutenant's wife. And though the stories seemed infinite in their digressions, the lick of the postmistress's eyes across a letter's address, the whistling of the vicar, the antics of a well-known flirt, the moggie's insistent needs would flash here and there in the narrative and so anchor them in that world, enfolding them in a landscape as different as could be imagined from that wasted stretch, No Man's Land, where anything that had been distinctive was blown away or mashed to bits and merged with the amorphous mud of battlefield, where indistinguishable limbs and fragments of clothing and equipment congealed into slimy walls of grey clay.

The irony that struck him all the time now was the pointlessness, the directionless quality of their days in trench. A push forward several yards, fifty or a hundred at most, and a retreat as much backwards. The uniformity of the landscape made every advance and every retirement insignificant. And yet it could end for any one of them at any moment. While the letters . . . in the letters was a world of lights and smells and soft air, and mists (without the ochre-green omen of gas), of the odors of sweet gale and lavender, baked puddings and blackcurrant cakes, an old-fashioned turf fire. But more than this, there was shifting scenery and incidents distinguished by their variety and eccentricity. It was not one death after another, deflating loss upon loss, erosion of body and spirit. It was plot and forward movement (without retiring behind lines) and surprise upon surprise, and for all that, for all its progress, it was never-ending, with no abrupt cutting off of wind and sunlight, but a hallowed succession of party-colored days with blooming and fading histories; it was not this suspension of time and lives.

The sergeant was only too glad for them to be relieved. Since Amiens, they'd hardly had a breather—twenty-two days on the line this last push to break the deadlock. Time for a bit of rest for all of them. (Let the Kiwis hold the line for now. Or bloody Yanks, the shirkers—Yanks and tanks were going to win this war, so they were always told. Well, he'd seen the ditched machines, even the light Whippets, stuck to their guns in mud, and he was fair certain he'd see the Americans in it as well.) For now, he hoped, rather than believed, that the lieutenant would come to himself with some rest, with a bit of plonk in some estaminet, with the company of some pretty French memselles, and the companionship of other officers.

They tramped the narrow and crooked maze of communication trenches back to the hut that the swank liked to call Battalion Headquarters. The quartermaster-sergeant made a pantomime of distributing the latest post, sniffing and rolling his eyes at each letter addressed to someone in their mob. The men tolerated this buffoonery to avoid a dust-up, and as soon as all the mail was spoken for, each man of Pearce's lot moved off to shuffle through his own limp bits of paper and sodden, brown-wrapped parcels, in search of her writing. The few who hadn't got letters from the lieutenant's wife solaced themselves with the ones they carried about, rubbed through with wear, reminding Pearce of the precious silver paper Agnes's mam had kept her wedding veil in, yellowed, but still as beautiful, he'd thought, as the veil itself. Rather than chance losing them, the men entrusted these fragile treasures to the sergeant while they stripped for delousing. It occurred to him that the letters were their own miracle, like the men who cherished them, flimsy stuff that managed to survive damp, rats, and violence. While he watched the lads caper about, making much of their bit of a bathe, he held the letters gingerly, resisting the urge to read them and fearful of tearing any. He was relieved to return them to their owners.

"Oi, Sergeant!" the post corporal, an annoying little cockney sparrow named Chandler, called to Pearce before he could turn away. The sergeant was never much for banter, but all the surviving NCOs of the battalion kept up a pretense of being mates—otherwise, their status, a kind of social limbo between officers and men, could cut them off entirely from human warmth. "I'd 'ave thought your lieutenant would want these, then, Colin, but 'e's not been 'ere for 'em."

"I'll bring him the lot, then, shall I, Alf?"

"'Ere, I danno, mate. It's me bloody arse if 'e comes lookin' for 'em. I'll be sent in again and blown ter fuckin' bits before yer can spit."

"Quit larkin' about, yer bleedin' git," retorted the sergeant, lapsing into Black Country in his irritation, "I'll bren 'em to 'im straightaway." He forced a smile. "Any road up, it's cushy enough in trench. Yer ought to spend some time there with us heroes."

Whatever they felt about this exchange, they slapped each other on the back and parted laughing.

Pearce crossed the miserable, shell-pitted drill ground with the letters pressed to his chest so that he would not have to look at them. It was that queer, now he thought of it—him with letters for everyone in his hands this day, everyone but himself, that is. He didn't care to have even these in his possession too long and he hurried to catch the lieutenant in his tent before he'd removed to officers' billets in the town.

A sorry mist spread over the valley encampment, like a reproach to their very presence there. Though he knew better, the sergeant always expected the mud and the damp to be exclusive to the trenches, the backdrop to the kind of evil done there. Snatches of song from the infantry huts drifted to him. ("Gassed last night, and gassed the night before" . . . "Oh, it's a lovely war" . . . "Hanging on the old barbed wire") Most of them were humorous, and many of them featured cook, sergeant-major and sergeant as villains. ("No more NCOs to curse me!") The effect should have been comical, but it depressed him. The words came heavy with wet through the foggy evening; though he couldn't enter the spirit of their black humor just then, he paused to listen, nevertheless.

> O, it's paradise at the parados.
> The whizzbangs fly o'er me head,

> And Jack Johnson leaves his card
> (He's a gennelman, by Gawd!).
> Oh, it's a cushy life for the dead!

At least this was one in which the sergeant didn't figure as a bully.

> There's boko shows at the parados,
> But the mud's soft under me head,
> And no bully beef for me,
> 'Cos I'm blown to buggery.
> Oh, it's a cushy life for the dead!

Some reedy Highland tenor was screeching out the chorus ("ta d*eeed*") like the very banshee, and the sergeant pulled his collar up around his ears and hunched over as he picked his way across camp to the tents.

The wet stuck to the lieutenant's tent, making the canvas sag as though hopeless. Pearce caught the murmur of voices within, and his shoulders relaxed—though he hadn't realized it, he'd been dreading this encounter since Chandler had handed him the letters. In trench, he'd grown uncomfortable in the company of the lieutenant and thought it would be worse here without the buffer of the men's presence. But if the lieutenant was easy conversing with his own, Pearce thought, then perhaps be he had been worrying for nothing. Perhaps their lieutenant had just been tired was all.

One lamp lighted the bell tent, meant to shelter four subalterns. Now only Captain Ashcroft and his batman were present, besides the lieutenant, and they were keeping voices low so as not to waken him where he lay prone on his cot with his face turned to the canvas. The captain and his orderly acknowledged the sergeant briefly and departed, probably to arrange some officers' small celebration in the town. The sergeant's spirits sank at their departure. Taking care to move quietly, he drew near the lieutenant's cot, intending to leave the letters where the lieutenant would find them when he woke. He was startled by the lieutenant's voice, low and terrifying.

"It's a shame about the foot, Sergeant. I am sorry."

"Sir?"

"One always likes to have something to bring back, don't you think?"

The sergeant's scalp tightened.

"I'm not sure what you mean, Lieutenant."

"I realize there is absolutely nothing left of poor Skinner, you know, but I tried. Truly I made every effort to find the foot."

"Not Sampson's foot, sir? When?"

By now Pearce had circled the cot, and he went rigid: to his dismay, he could see that the lieutenant was tracing patterns with this finger in the dirt and straw. Under the sergeant's stare, the officer stopped suddenly and sat up. Brushing his hands together, he stood and said, as though reassuring himself, "It will turn up."

Pearce was speechless. You couldn't tell *what*, never mind *who* you found after shelling or bombs most times, and you didn't bring home the scraps. You spread them with lime, when you could, and hoped there was nothing human left to recognize if you found yourself in the same line again. But never mind all that, they were at least forty miles and many months from abandoned Lewis-gun cart and its captive foot—why, even if they could reach it, the rats would've had it by now.

The lieutenant spotted the letters in Pearce's hands, took them from him and patted him on the shoulder.

"Going into the town with your mates tonight? Corporal Chandler and the two Geordie sergeants are expecting you to join them, I think."

When his sergeant didn't answer, the lieutenant smiled and turned to leave, but he stopped abruptly, looking distressed.

"Oh, look . . . oh," he said, "I've got them filthy."

Some of the grime from his hands had smeared itself across the top letter. Absently rubbing it with his sleeve, the lieutenant left the tent with the sergeant trembling inside it.

Chapter 5

As it turned out, they only had the one night in town before moving out to Valenciennes, and in less than a week, they were playing the game again. After the scene in the tent, Pearce had no hope of the lieutenant coming round to sharing the letters again, and in fact, the readings stopped entirely.

Of course, discussion of the lieutenant's letters had faltered as his readings fell off, but each man had his own cache to read and re-read, and each kept his letters close to his chest. The letter-less sergeant woke from fitful sleeps with a clutching at his heart. He woke always groping for his gun, even in reserve, with a sense of having been stripped of protection. It was even worse in support trench, where he woke to find the lieutenant silently staring into the shadows with empty eyes. Their first night forward on the assault line, they sank in muddy water to their knees before their feet got purchase on the duckboards. On this night, the sergeant woke in dugout to find the lieutenant's eyes on himself.

"Sergeant." The lieutenant spoke to him in a whisper. They had just suffered a particularly unnerving assault, and most of the men were dozing or fingering their letters in the dark. McMichael and Worrall could be heard discussing the level of bombardment ("A medium that, laddie" . . . "Pull t'other 'un, mate—it was a soddin' heavy, I'm tellin' yeh.") Pearce glanced down the trench in their direction before answering, "Yes, sir."

"I have to go out."

A wave of panic broke over the sergeant and he began to sweat furiously. He stifled an impulse to call out to the others.

"Have we orders, sir?"

"I'll be back before daylight. I'm leaving you in charge here." With that, the lieutenant slipped over so quickly and soundlessly that the sense of his presence lingered after him like a ghost.

The sergeant hurried to the first man along the trench, the sentry on the left flank fire-step where the trench traversed suddenly forward to a sap. The man had his back to him and was hard to distinguish in the dark. He turned the lad around.

"Who is it?"

"Craddock, Sergeant. I'm not asleep!"

"Corporal Craddock, take over the men. I'm over it, then."

"Wha—you can' do that, Sergeant! I'm not corporal. Bolton is. Or give Worrall the leg up. I'm not corporal material, as they say—"

"As they say, Craddock, too bloody bad. There's no time—I'm after the lieutenant."

Craddock clawed at the sergeant's tunic.

"He's never out there? On his own? Not on his own in the bleedin' mud?"

"Just keep it together until we're back in trench, understand? And keep quiet about it."

The muck was vicious to crawl through. The sucking sound it made gave away his position at every moment. And it made him sick with fear to have his head this close to it, remembering tales of those sucked into sink holes made by the shell craters at Passchendaele. When soft enough, he'd been told, they'd been quicksand and could drag a man down entirely before his mates knew he'd gone. This was no Passchendaele, but there were crump holes here, too, and a wounded man could still drown in shallow mud. The lads were too attuned to one another now for these pits to pose a serious threat, but the thought of them in the lieutenant's path made the sergeant's throat catch in panic. There was no thread of psychic connection between him and the officer, not like whatever it was linked the others. His instinct had fled him, and he felt himself floundering forward hopelessly in the direction he had seen the man disappear.

So it surprised him to spot the lieutenant so quickly, an infinitesimally darker blotch against the dark and blotchy landscape. But the officer's movements were confusing. He gave the impression of a grazing animal, a bullock hunched and bobbing gently at the earth as he cropped first this patch and then another. The sergeant scanned the distance for evidence of the Jerry line, then crouched and approached the lieutenant cautiously. It remained difficult to distinguish anything more than the humped dark form and the bobbing motion until he was almost on top of the man. The lieutenant was groping along the mud, patting the earth silently with both hands and feeling each irregularity carefully until resuming the movement a few inches farther along. Blind, he looked blind . . . or mad.

The air left the sergeant's body in a rush of horror, and an icy spasm ran up his back. He knew, he knew without asking, the lieutenant was looking for Sampson's foot.

The sergeant crawled up alongside his officer. The lieutenant gave him a dazed glance before continuing to search.

"We must get back to trench, sir, the lads'll miss us soon."

The lieutenant sighed heavily. " 'Swift as quicksilver, it courses through the natural gates and alleys of the body—' "

"Fritz'll hear us, Lieutenant. We must move now. Back to trench."

" '. . . and a most instant'—something—'tetter,' I think, 'bark'd about' . . . 'bark'd about with vile and loathsome crust all my smooth body . . . my smooth body,' Sergeant."

"Yes, sir."

The sergeant had his arms around him now and was gathering him as gently as he could in an awkward dragging motion toward their line.

"It's *Hamlet*, Sergeant, do you know it?"

"Thought it was Shakespeare, yes, sir."

The lieutenant disengaged himself from Pearce, and now the two were side by side, pulling themselves slowly through the mud on elbows and bellies. A thin fillet of dawn was just visible in the grey air to the east. The sergeant urged the lieutenant on. They could actually see the edge of the trench; it meant they could be seen as well.

When they were a few yards short of safety, a sniper's bullet pinged against the rim of the sergeant's helmet and he flattened himself, pulling the lieutenant down with him. A box perisher peeping over the parapet told him that Craddock was anxiously watching their progress.

The lieutenant's head was next to his and faced away from him. He squeezed the officer's shoulder, he wasn't certain what for—encouragement, maybe. The man turned his head to look at the sergeant.

This time he appeared to see *him,* Pearce, and not just through him, as had been the case for so long. This time Pearce could see his own presence register in the lieutenant's eyes, along with something bewildering— pity. Then before the sergeant knew what was happening, the lieutenant rose, turned toward the Hun line, took a volley of sniper bullets in the head and chest and sank onto the sergeant, who was still lying flat, his face only some feet from Craddock and the men.

It was November 2, 1918. Nine days later, the war ended, and the platoon returned to a cautious welcome, a hero's welcome, but tinged with suspicion about the fact that they were all there, all but the very early mates and the lieutenant.

Part II

Chapter 6

. . . gray plain all round:
Nothing but plain to the horizon's bound.
I might go on, naught else remained to do.

So, on I went. I think I never saw
Such starved ignoble nature, nothing throve. . .
—from "Childe Roland to the Dark Tower Came,"
by Robert Browning

(Southampton, 1918)

They'd been dazed, all of them, since the lieutenant's death, and the war's end, and homecoming, each event hard on the heels of the one before, leaving them no time to gather their thoughts. Rumors came to them of the sad irony of lads in other regiments, some distracted like themselves, some simply blindsided in the midst of their relief and joy by fatal accidents after the fighting stopped. But they knew that they were destined to return together, to survive even that sly assassin, the Spanish influenza, which would take so many others in the warm counterpanes of their beds at home or the blued and boiled sheets of their hospital cots. They knew this, and so they expressed no surprise at the plans for their orchestrated arrival home, the entire platoon (so it would be printed) stepping off the ship as one to the frenzy of the crowd and the pumping of the military band. It was arranged that they would emerge together like heroes.

It was the dazed state, not the light really—there was little on that grey afternoon—that made them appear to blink like voles as they edged nervously around and through the general euphoria. They were mustered out there on the spot for the occasion, to avoid the anti-climax of traveling on to the Midlands or some other center for the official discharge. It was another privilege which set them apart from the rest, made them uneasy among their own.

The War Office had gone to the trouble to invite their families to meet them and had actually provided an accurate date, if not the hour itself, and so some were taken away, after speeches were made and honors distributed, by their dads and mams and sweethearts and a few by wives. Some fewer still had children run to meet them. Some wandered away on their own. They all darted quick questioning looks at one another before fragmenting, picked off one after the other as if by snipers, as they would never have allowed themselves to be on the other side. Here the surge of welcome was too much for them, and since they weren't chums really, since they were all strangers to one another, really and truly now they came to think of it, at least among their own, they yielded as they would never have done on the front. Bolton, Craddock, Mabb, Dixon, Worrall . . . they all became hats or heads bobbing along helplessly as the tide took them.

None of them posed or smiled, or looked that he felt a hero, and it was that aura, of worry or despair or the simple weight of experience and memory, that made the occasion seem not right and the sheer jaw-dropping fact of their having beaten the odds so spectacularly to take on a suspicion of something other than bravery and dumb luck.

Pearce's Agnes hadn't come. They'd had an understanding right from the start of the war: she was never to meet him at the boat, nor the station, nor visit him in hospital or find him in London; she was never to expect him, never to waylay him. On leaves, and the once he had returned wounded, whenever he had time and opportunity enough to go to her, he did: he wanted always to find her again in her dad's shop, as he had the first time he saw her, surrounded by the things that made a framework around her in his mind—pieces of timber and spindles and iron tyres and the lathe for turning the spokes. He'd first noticed her because of her dad's spokes. Whimsical, they were. He recognized them straight off after that when he'd see them on milk carts and wagonettes, often painted whimsical, as well. That was how he liked to see her, though he didn't explain it that way to her. (Pearce's Agnes, it turned out, was not whimsical.) He only told her don't meet him, and never a sentimental wench, she agreed her dad could hardly spare her for that, for meeting him, even if she knew where he'd be, when, after all, he was on his way home, wasn't he? That was early days, that promise, but it stood him right now, for she'd not come, even to this celebration. And he was relieved not to have her there, for he'd anticipated, as the other lads had not, the sea of eager faces, the bewildering rush and color and unfamiliar noises banging against their ears that still missed the soft syllables of the lieutenant's voice. And he didn't want to be absorbed by all that, by that and by his wife's relief and love, not yet . . . not until he'd read them all.

For the sergeant had inherited (so to speak) the letters. He who had received not one from the lieutenant's wife came into possession after the lieutenant's death of all of them, old and new and those the lieutenant had kept to himself and never read aloud. He'd found them mostly intact, carefully tied into bundles with bits of string and bootlaces, the lot of them folded in a large swathe of rubberized cloth cut from an army rain cape, to keep out the wet and the rats. It surprised him and it didn't: surprised him that the lieutenant had had it in him to carry and protect them to the end, and then didn't because of what they were. He meant to return them to her himself. But he meant to read them first, every one of them in order before he gave them up. And then he meant to see her. Beyond that, he couldn't have said what his plans were.

He scattered some words to the newspapermen and then picked his way among his men, fracturing into strangers now before the sergeant's eyes without the lieutenant to weave through them like a strand through pearls. He gave a squeeze here and there to a shoulder he never expected to see again, a smile of forced heartiness to their families; they ducked their heads and he turned his, all of them avoiding the direct look, wary of betraying too much, afraid they'd never be able to finish this thing that they'd started—their homecoming, their lives again. And then he had his own guilty cargo to carry and to keep, even from them. He quickened his pace, worried they would sense them, the letters in his pack, and challenge him, as he had thought they might challenge him in the days after the lieutenant's death.

(And this stealth and sliding of eyes contributed to the suspicions of the newspapermen, who threw their heads back and cast knowing looks at one another, but would still write words like "vanquished the foe" and "heroically fought against tremendous odds" and "battled past fear and exhaustion for the glory of their Country.")

Once he'd left the crowd behind, he fairly flew to the trains. If he'd not been so frightened at himself, he could have hugged himself to think of his destination. The very place of his dreams, of all their longings, the lieutenant's wife's village! He knew her evening walk and the dairy and the dale, its hedges and low stone walls, in minute detail, as though he'd grown up a rural lad there and run mail for her from the wickedly curious postmistress and sung evensong with a boys choir to Alphaeus the musical vicar's quivering joy. He saw that sweet man's shining pale face, unlined and innocent as a baby's, and the shadow of the supple Leach lurking behind him. He imagined himself let in by Mrs. Lanton, and Moggie shooting out past his feet the instant the door was open, and then "Pussums, Pussums . . . I'm sorry, sir, only she's a pet you know," and the bright—was it? no, she'd be in mourning, damn!—the *sad* voice of the letter-writer, the lieutenant's Emma: "Who is it, Mrs. Lanton? Please show our visitor here to me . . ."

He started reading them on the train, crowded as it was and dirty, too, smuts everywhere. It was not a troop special, though it might as well have been, it was so crammed with soldiers heading north for the de-mob center, worse than leave traffic. By the time it left the station, eleven men—none of them his lot, he made certain—were packed into a third-class compartment designed to carry eight. It should have bothered him, but from the first impress of her pen on the salutation of the earliest letter, he was absorbed, delighting in the letters that predated the lieutenant's coming to them, nervous and elated that he alone would have these, that he was their only living reader. They might have been addressed to him for all anyone knew, and he touched with his fingers the endearments with which she ended every letter and which the Lieutenant had kept to himself. He touched them to feel the pulse beneath the words, as he had longed to do so often in trench.

"She wrote you summat, then, Sarge, din' she?"

"Yeh'll soon be holdin' the real thing, then, eh, Sarge?"

"Your missus 'as a lot ter say, doesn' she, Sarge? Get a word in, does you?"

He scowled them silent and stuffed the letters away. Though never one for pretending, he feigned sleep—and really did sleep.

He slept through the Midlands where Agnes waited for him, and where those around him must have detrained for mustering out. He slept through Sheffield, and Doncaster, and woke at York, finally, for a wait and a change of lines for her village. Arrived there at last and collecting himself quickly, he swung down in the gathering dark to the platform.

The train hissed behind him as he took in his surroundings. He was profoundly dismayed to find the place had a cold, grimed feel to it. Beyond the station house, he could see the dark silhouettes of a few abject naked trees dotting the greying horizon in a way that was familiar and nightmarish. He looked for the station sign to assure himself that he had the right stop and then walked stiffly to the master's window. That unhealthy-looking official sat before a supper of what appeared to be a gristly pasty and cider, which he had spread on the newspaper he was reading.

"I'm looking for a house." He turned over the topmost letter and pointed to the return address.

The station master looked at it with a heavy, resigned melancholy.

"Aye. Just 't'other side of dairy."

"Is it a long walk?"

The man looked at his uniform.

"Tha'd be wanting t' widow."

"Yes. I'm—"

"Lieutenant's batman, aye? Testimonial?"

Pearce felt himself redden. Not his bloody servant, no, he thought, his . . . his what? He paused, gave a quick nod. "Yeh. That's right. But thought I'd look in tomorrow. Is there a place to stay the night?"

"T'are 'n 'Ounds, just right not twenty paces, do thee a cold supper. But tha'll not be looking in tomorrow—there's a train out again in another two hours."

"I'm not leaving right away."

"But widow's not there, Sergeant. Left for Northumbria, on t'sea, so they say—she 'ales fra thereabouts."

The sergeant's heart sank. "Did she? When was that?"

"Just missed 'er—yesterday." The little man removed what was left of his meal from the newspaper and brushed off the crumbs. Finding what he wanted, he folded the paper and handed it to Pearce.

"Thought she might nip on down t'greet your lads, but she couldn't face 'em, I expect. Miracle, tha', eh? All o' you surviving like tha'?" There was even in this lethargic man's tone that hum of suspicion with which people would greet his reputation for heroism for the rest of his life. And, as he would for the rest of his life, the sergeant kept silent. No one deserved it from him. Not one of them deserved an explanation, except herself.

Pearce skimmed the article. They had managed to include a murky photograph of the lads—he could hardly recognize himself—at the Rouen rail station, alongside a clearer one of the lieutenant in mufti, fresh-faced and even younger than the sergeant remembered him coming to them. The headline read, "Charmed Platoon Survive Years of Battle Intact (Officer Sole Casualty)." "Charmed." He handed it back. They had failed to take Sampson and Skinner into account.

"What time's the first train out tomorrow, then?"

"Be un for York leaves 6:43, change a' Doncaster for Berwick-a'-Tweed; 'tis coast all t'way fra Newcastle— tha's Berwick . . . Upon . . . Tweed, aye, tha's almost Scotland, tha'. She's two stops back fra there. Sure to be sumon give you a lift fra station."

"6:43. Ta. I'll be here." He started for the inn, but wheeled around at a thought.

"Is there no one then at the house?" He hesitated before suggesting, "Mrs. Lanton?"

The man eyed him keenly.

"No, she's closed it up for new family. There's nowt there now."

The sergeant didn't know how to ask about the cat, and it ate at him as he made for the Hare's glowing windows. If it had been daylight still, he would have chanced an adventure, would have found his own way, he was certain, would have crossed the fields by the dairy and seen the house as he approached from the thicket where she had stepped on one of the debauched artist's empty bottles and twisted her ankle—would it still be sore even now? And he thought of it, slim, bandaged, throbbing as she leant back in her favorite chair and wished she could walk again. He would try the door—and if it opened to him, call gently, "Moggie, Moggie . . ." or "Puss Puss," probably, as the cat was used to Mrs. Lanton, he remembered. Just to assure himself that Moggie was gone, too, and was all right, was not abandoned in the place and frantic. He didn't like cats as pets—they were for barns and stables and cellars. They were mousers and ratters, weren't they, really? Workers. Not pets. But he wouldn't feel right until he'd made sure of the moggie. For her sake.

Now, even knowing she wasn't there, he played with the idea of staying on a day—to check the house for Moggie. And to walk in her paths, meet her neighbors and guess their identities before they opened their mouths. He would see the vicar Alphaeus and watch the soft man's face go all dewy with emotion as he tried to restrain the tears that came at the thought of the lieutenant's death and the widow's decamping . . .

Chapter 7

It still wasn't late in the evening when Pearce approached the Hare and Hounds, and as he passed the lighted windows of the pub, the sounds from within told him it was fairly full and lively. His hand was on the public house door when he suffered a sensation of complete loneliness: he could have been on the moon, he thought, for all the places—station and inn—where he'd been in her world, since neither of these had figured at all in her letters. He resisted the urge for a pint; the thought of so many ungenerous eyes turning on him as he entered oppressed his morale. A sigh of misgiving seemed to have followed him from France, and he knew all too well how guilt, the wrong guilt, would be read in his face.

He knew now that he would leave in the morning. For even if she hadn't taken all color and vitality with her when she left, even if morning breathed beauty into this sodden and black-washed landscape, without her, he had no passport into her enchanted land. Dressed in army kit, he would be like some goblin let loose in faerydom. His touch might turn it all to dust.

He strode past the tavern door to the inn's entrance, determined to settle in immediately and read the letters— all of them, if it took all night and the next day in the trains, so he would have had them all before he met her.

He arranged for a room—the cheapest, he was made to understand, unless he agreed to share a bed, and the innkeeper looked him up and down suspiciously when he insisted on a private chamber. He paid in advance and followed the upstairs girl to a room backing onto an over-fragrant stable. There was a bed, a chamber pot and a basin on a rickety stand—no fire and no electric—and the bed was small, maybe even meant for a child, but he didn't plan to sleep. Pretending to high spirits he didn't feel, he chivvied the girl for an extra candle ("there's a good wench"); he wanted to be sure of the light as he'd a night of reading before him.

Dearest Richard,

What you say about your young men, "the lads," you know, it makes me think of when I was a little girl and my father kept a hunter at Allen's Crosse Farm. It was a great expense for him, but apotheosized him, in a manner of speaking, into that godlike thing, a "maistorrr" in the eyes, at least, of Pick Wardner, old Allen's stableman from the beginning of time. There was something so quaint in the respect this old man paid my father, who could not have been more than thirty-five at the time. It wasn't servile, exactly, but filial, like a son, as though my father were his father, too, and would look after him—is that feudal, do you think?—though we were hardly in a position to do anything for the man were he to come a cropper.

It was a different kind of obeisance from the duck and pump hat-tipping and murmured "Morrin, Mister," he got throughout the village. It was love, really. Do I sound as completely stupid as I feel saying this? But it was love.

You couldn't have left us at a better time. Better for you, I mean, for what are German guns to the advent of a new cook? I'm sorry, my dear, is that frivolous? I'm groping for a tone, for you know, I'm afraid my longing will ooze from between the lines. Sorry, sorry, sorry, sorry.

Mrs. Lanton, you may remember because you took to her so, is my late Aunt Eliza's godmother, fallen on hard times, as they say. So she speaks well, and, as you perceived, she's amiable, not bitter, as was Mamie's great aunt in the same circumstances, and I dare say the odor is misleading. I'll find the right time and approach for mentioning it to her, if it's still with her, that is. I never really considered not hiring her, as she has a warm temperament, but I was bound to notice the aroma, and it is such an anomaly. She comes to me a week Sunday. So that's settled. It's a good thing, too, for the Cragg daughter's blackened toast is difficult to choke down, and she overcooks the mash. It is sitting rather heavily at the moment. (Taking advantage of my ignorance of local ways, she says it's meant to be Yorkshire "mushy mash," like mushy peas, I think.) Alphaeus asks me to tea or a meal quite often in pity for me, but I'm afraid the county will talk, so I only accept when there are others present, preferably of our wit. Otherwise, it can be so dull.

I don't think young men should be so handsome in uniform as they are, Richard. It makes goodbyes all the more difficult. They should be grimed and toothless and spit sidewise to punctuate a point, and then their women will think, "Good riddance to the idle lout! Jerry can have 'im, for all I care." Wives would send them off with glee.

What am I saying? There are wives who do that now. In fact, I witnessed a white feathering in town (I should never have lingered. Shopping? Whatever for? I've no one to impress now you're away), and it made my blood boil. You understand. I think the man was weak in the head, though I'm sure the ladies thought he was playing at madness, that he knew a hawk, etc. He had that baby face you see on men whose minds haven't grown older with them. But they reviled him and put the feather in his buttonhole, and he stroked it and smiled idiotically. I had to turn away.

Shall I write the War Office on the uniform issue? Another madwoman, will they think, and set me to knitting balaclava helmets?

It wasn't just old Pick who loved my father like that, as you know. Everyone did. I did. I never knew anyone to garner love like that, until you came along. And both of you, Dad and yourself, you loved me most. Must stop now. Treacherous tears imminent. Miss you, miss you, miss you.

Your Emma

P.S. I'll write as soon as I can about how things turn out with Mrs. Lanton. It keeps me in a welter of anticipation. What will happen next? What will happen?

A postscript! Kept alive at first by a mere postscript! He fought down a lump of distress and wiped his face, becoming conscious of how freely he was sweating, though the room was cold enough to crystallize his breath. It was just like in trench and him holding his doom in his hand, this letter with no story, nothing to anticipate . . . until the hint in the postscript. "The lads"—

they must have been from the North Riding Fusiliers, where the lieutenant had led a platoon before joining the sergeant's mob. They were most of them dead, the sergeant knew. Had the lieutenant not shared the letters with those poor buggers? Had they never known the bright entry into her world, the promise?

Dearest Richard,

Of course, I'll describe them. And your precious dales, if you like, though you know them as well as I. And what do you mean my "unique vision"? I see them plainly as they are! Perhaps with a hint of romance, yes. But I don't embellish, don't say so! I like things beautiful, but plainly so—am I contradicting? You are plainly beautiful, no fuss, no embellishments, just strong limbs and fresh blue eyes and fine long fingers. And funny feet—yes, they are!

I've a kitten! Did I say? No, I can't have because I hadn't a kitten last time I wrote. Audrey disapproves, though she's been on about the mice for as long as I can remember (well, there is fur everywhere) and she insists on replacing those awful antimacassars to protect against the wee thing's tiny claws! But I won't have them! I detest antimacassars. And I will have the cat. Mrs. Lanton is with me on this (she thinks me lonely). I think you must have left it for me to find. Did you? It's our kitten, then, I make it so. Our moggie. Must think of a name, but everything has associations somehow. I'll wait to see what kind of personality it will have. It's got that universal kitten disposition right at the moment— all frisk and flash.

You wanted to know about Mrs. Lanton's encounter with Willis the butcher. She was quite red-faced about the chop, I think I told you. For the life of me I couldn't detect the odor she described.

Oh, but wait, I get ahead of myself. I'm still not very good at this—do you think Scheherazade had to reverse herself and pick up where she'd left out something, a detail, you know, that was necessary to one of her stories? How unnerving it would have been for her, poor girl, as her life depended on being entertaining.

Well, here is my dropped detail. At the time I agreed to let Mrs. Lanton "deal with" Mr. Willis, I still had not confronted her about her own odor. I had rehearsed all manner of such confrontation: humorous ("Dear Mrs. Lanton, just because we live in the country, it is not necessary to maintain quite so much of a stable aura about one"); contrite ("I am so sorry to have to bring this up, and please believe that I am more embarrassed to have to mention it than you could ever . . . blah blah blah"); blasé ("Oh, by the way, Mrs. Lanton, I made the most unfortunate purchase in town the other day—a full liter of French eau de toilette—for the bath, you know; it just doesn't suit me, but I thought you might . . ."); wheedling ("It's a little eccentricity of my own, my dear Mrs. Lanton, but I beg you to indulge me . . ."); perhaps turning confessional ("It comes, no doubt, of the time my puppy died under the nursery floor and wasn't discovered until he had become quite mummified and the nursery had become forever associated in my mind with crypts and ghouls!"). I put hours of recitation into preparing for the much-dreaded discussion. But whenever I had the opportunity to speak about it—well, all I had to do was remove myself from the situation and imagine it as you must imagine it where you are, and you can see, can't you, how ridiculous it seemed? My chin would begin to wobble with the ludicrousness of the whole thing, and I let the moment slip by me.

So, it was enveloped in this very vivid scent and bearing with indignation the meat with its phantom smell that our Mrs. Lanton set off to the village. I should never have let her go in such ironic circumstance, and to add to my unease, the weather began to cloud over, just as it does in cinema when the villain is at large or a disaster at hand. Everything conspired, as you can tell, to warn me against letting Mrs. L loose on Mr. W.

I am surprised you did not hear the sounds of their confrontation even where you are, surrounded and deafened by guns, as the papers tell us. It really must have seemed to the others present like the end of the world. I got the story from Lavinia Pratt. She was badgering Mr. Willis for lamb again ("with a <u>war</u> on, Missus?"). She does spoil Alphaeus horribly. In his defense, though, he has asked her to respect Mr. W's patriotism, but she's a believer in the old precedence of the clergy, and Alphaeus couldn't have a more vigorous campaigner on his side than that old housekeeper. Lavinia must already have put Willis in a ripe old mood when in blew Mrs. Lanton, like Nelson's fleet with cannon ablaze . . .

It was one of her best. As he had forgotten to expect, and as delighted him, it explained later references in the letters the lieutenant read to him and the men on the front. He now knew, for instance, why a packet of soup bones had arrived at the kitchen addressed—with some irony—as a gift to Mrs. Lanton and with violets pinned to the string. And why later, Mrs. Lanton said that in spite of their suffering for scarcity of meat, she "wouldn't set foot again in a foul charnel house like Willis's!"

They were rich food these early letters, rich and filling, offering several varied narratives only partially familiar to him from such later references. But as much as he enjoyed these treats, he was still eager to get to the end—to the last line of the letter, or often the last few—for the endearments, sentimental and sensual and warm with conjured embrace.

He read deep into the night, breaking only once to stand in the open window and exhale the smoke from his cigarette into the yard below, forcing himself to shake the feeling that the ember tip was a sniper's delight. He could hear the thudding hooves of dreaming horses and sense the stealth of stable cats. A dull moon seemed to dodge among the cloud masses, too dim and erratic to read by. By the time it was swallowed up altogether and a greasy drizzle began, he had finished his cigarette. He turned back to the letters. There were scores and scores of them, of course, and his progress was hampered by his needing to linger over them, but he skimmed the ones he remembered from trench, relishing only the endearments, making them his. Just before a sulfuric yellow dawn crept up over the stables, he could hear the house waking to its daily needs. Doors slammed, light footsteps brushed down the hall. He divided the letters into two piles, those he had finished making the vastly larger one, and the other, it broke his heart to realize, of possibly three dozen—no more. He crossed to the washstand and splashed some icy water on his face, grateful there was no mirror to send him back a wry or doubtful self, a punished face, a hapless pretender to the lieutenant.

He'd had no dinner the day before, no tea and very little supper, but he took no breakfast at the inn. The girl, who blushed now when he smiled at her, wrapped a slab of cheese and some black bread in paper so he could slip away without attracting notice.

Chapter 8

The day began dark, and he retained the sense of bleakness, as though he'd only gone back to support or reserve lines, and not home, not to her country. Resisting a last urge to explore her world, he pulled himself aboard the train for a juddering ride from hamlet to hamlet until he gained York, then Doncaster again and the North Eastern's line to Scotland. At Newcastle, he had to choose between a compartment of nervous returning Geordies and Scots (duty-bound cheerfulness writ unpersuasively across broad, freckled faces) and that inhabited by one old woman. The old gran made him think of Mrs. Lanton, though this woman sitting in the third-class carriage couldn't be anything like that resourceful cook and housekeeper. (Hadn't the lieutenant's wife said Mrs. Lanton'd been gentry once, or nearly so?) Still, he entered her compartment and sat across from her. She lapsed into a snoring peace as soon as the train began moving.

Why, here was Stonecroft described for the first time! He laughed aloud at the discovery, almost wakening the old woman.

He is a burly chap. He has the look of one who, finding his face in the glass one morning to resemble that of an ancient mariner or Gil Blas's wise old hermit, was forced to abandon the sensitive youth attitude which must have won him the comfort of many a Parisian lady's bosom and has adopted the volatile Old Sage of the Dales persona, shaking his blackthorn at trespassers, who amount these days to tiny 'Becca Uttley and her cows ambling to and from pasture.

As for 'Becca herself, who was little more than a baby when you could have last seen her, it is a mystery to me how that small child coaxes her beasts, any one of whom could cut short that quick sprite's life with a single good kick. She is a nervous little thing, fussing and worrying the kye, and though she has been warned, will take the wood copse cut. The wee stretch of it which passes before Stonecroft's hovel has been forbidden her by that worthy painter, who considers it his own. For all of her timidity among the beasts, she is a Tartar to Stonecroft, and the blasphemies that confront one another from the mouths of the babe and the man are enough to make one dizzy. Stonecroft insists, to anyone who will listen, that she is a changeling and violates his sense of property in order to confuse his mind and steal his creative soul. He offers as proof the fact that she always appears with what he calls the "phantom herd" when the sun is yet a pale finger in the east and then at gloaming, times when spirits are known to slip in and out of the shadows, making one brush one's hand across one's eyes and wonder if one is seeing things. The fact that these are also the times when one moves one's herd escapes him for all his posing as a bucolic sage.

Dear sweet Alphaeus, however, is convinced of Stonecroft's rustic expertise and is forever asking his opinion on the proper way to strain curd, when to start herbs in indoors to avoid the frost, etc., while the old fraud, when confronted with such a test, either adopts his laconic genius role, refusing to engage in what he terms "social palaver," or (if he be in his cups!) waxes eloquent on the soul-expanding properties of the rural life and the satisfaction of living off the land. I don't think he has ever spent more than a week out of London or Paris until arriving here, and the formidable postmistress Sturgess's conclusion concerning his residence among us (unkind, of course) is that he became a country gentleman out of fear of the zeppelins.

Mrs. Lanton, a village woman herself, is forever sending him little treats, which he accepts with an uncomfortable sidewise glance and gruff laugh. I'm sure he doesn't know what to make of what she calls her trifle, but when I suggested that she warn him about the rather imaginative substitutions for cream and eggs, she huffed a bit and said, "A gentleman like Mr. Stonecroft will know how to shift in times of privation, since he has lived as a hermit all his life."

These conflicting interpretations of Stonecroft's character make for some tense words between the Sturgess and our Mrs. L. The postmistress has been heard to say, with an air of knowing what's what, "That one's got her skirts in a twist over His Nibs, the old pretender."

If little 'Becca is present at such a pronouncement, she is liable to cock her head to hear better the judgment of her elders on the man whom she calls "t'ol' bugger in t'wood."

He stopped another snort of laughter and turned to the final paragraph. But, where he had come to expect and relish words of intimate assurance, he found something else.

Don't be annoyed, please, my love, but your letters grow shorter and shorter, and darker and darker, and I don't know what to make of most of the references. You used to quote me poetry—the old bard of the Lakes, and nonsense rhyme, and lovely Robbie Burns.

And I laughed so heartily at the irreverent songs you overheard the men sing, particularly the one about "the rag-time company." I can't show them to anyone, of course; Mrs. Lanton, not to mention Alphaeus, would be scandalized!

I'm troubled now, though. What do you mean about the Whizzbang song (or poem, is it?) and both wanting and fearing sleep, "like Hamlet's sleep—it is what keeps me going, that the sleep may actually be worse that the waking"? You will come home to me, my beautiful boy, my darling, you will, you will.

Recalling lines of dismal lyrics ("a cushy life for the dead") making their way through the mist-laden French night to lie heavily on his heart, Pearce tried not to be angry with the lieutenant for having subjected her, even obliquely like this, to his inner darkness. But he soon forgot the passage in the next letter's return to Stonecroft.

Your Mr. Bradshaw, who wonders frequently about shortages at home, will want to know how our Stonecroft manages to procure so much good whiskey, and really, I can't say. We as a nation are all counseled by placard and handbill to banish Demon Drink, which I think Mr. Lloyd George considers a graver threat than the Germans. I'm afraid that there is rather more of it about here than your men are able to enjoy, though pious Lavinia Pratt is always after Alphaeus to write the Ministry about the evil of your own rum ration. I wanted to send you some of that lovely brandy your uncle left you in that funny will of his, but a distraught Phyllis Whitehead told me that an enormous cake she had procured from Fortnum's and a small bottle of sherry never reached her Captain in France. I do remember, though, something I heard at infirmary last Thursday: a sister was remarking how some wonderful friend of hers conceived the plan of hiding a bottle in a loaf of stale bread to send to her son at the front, so that the parcel would have no appeal for anyone who came upon it. But I am afraid to take the chance with Uncle's brandy, and you did say that it will last some time without opening, so I shan't try it, shall I?

This was all until—what he'd been expecting, dreading, really—another hint of something gone wrong. Reading it, he recalled his first moment of alarm, when the lieutenant had laughed in that ugly way.

Richard, don't read this aloud. I don't know how to ask. Am I imagining things? Your letters have changed. I know you don't like to write about yourself, but only about the men, or the small moments of poetry that come to you. But you write less and less of even these. And the things you do write are worrisome to me. What do you mean to say about the Childe Roland poem? I've looked for it in your library and cannot find it. Can you quote some of it for me? You left me with rather a dark impression of your thoughts, my dear. What can I do?

Are my letters too stupid? Not stupid enough? How can I cheer you? Will you not share what grieves you?

Forgive me, my dearest, but I love you more than my life. I had thought my silly tales of the people here were a balm to you. Have I failed in this? Shall I send the brandy? Or anything else that would cheer you? Please write to me one of our private letters again. I love you. I close my eyes and run my hands over your face, my beautiful lad. If I will it so, I will send my fingertips abroad to you—can you sense them? On your eyes, your chest? Shall I slip my hands beneath your tunic and press you to me?

If her blank fear called up waves of dread in him, the impetuous sensuality of its ending left him gasping. What had that bloody man written her to upset her like this?

The plucky waif 'Becca made a bright appearance in several letters; Stonecroft, too, of course, and many of the regulars among the denizens of the village, all of these personalities interwoven with a kind of gentle, lacy binding in the form of the generous-hearted vicar. There was no repetition of her black doubts, but a sombering of the tone overall. There was the same satiric archness, softened with genuine amusement at the antics of her neighbors, but there was also an increasing, sad notice of the sufferings around her. She had only rarely recorded the dire events of life in her earlier letters, and only when they so influenced her narrative that she could not neglect them. Now the deaths and disappointments seemed to gather themselves to her, and this new element in her voice, although restrained, was something altogether bleak and depressing.

For one thing, there was the recurrent anxiety over the diphtheria, which was making its way through the Riding, even the fresh country dales, taking children from their mothers as unpredictably and with as little compassion as a shelling. The Uttley children took ill with it, but death (thank God, thank the bloody fates, or country doctoring, thought the sergeant as he gripped the edges of the paper tightly), death did not claim them; they all survived, though little 'Becca's lungs and heart were affected. It was, she wrote to her lieutenant, "quite bad." She tried to convey a humorous picture of the anxious Stonecroft bringing the little girl a precious orange and pretty presents to amuse her while she lay, brows knit, in pet about the cows being brought in by one of the littler lads. She tried to capture Stonecroft, face alight, emptying a palmful of prize horehound lozenges into the child's lap. Stonecroft patiently holding the tiny hand while the doctor scraped the scum from a throat which spat out, between scrapes, the most unlikely curses and threats. But the humor was off, and the letter left the sergeant flat.

The last bundle had dwindled to half-dozen letters. There was even less of Stonecroft and nothing of Alphaeus in the next one, each missive shorter than the last and punctuated by her distress. He shot a glance at the old woman, who was snoring deeply and intently across from him, her basket at an awkward pitch from her lap, its kerchief shivering in the rocking motion of the carriage.

I found the Childe Roland. What a horrid poem! How is distresses me to think of you murmuring it to yourself (you cannot be sharing it with those lads!) in your trench. Please, please, let me soothe you. For my sake, put away the Browning and that dreadful Dover Beach, my love. You know you never thought much of Arnold's poetry! These are things to share over a cold fowl and pudding together at Sunday tea, when the sun is shining and can dispel the gloom. We used to laugh to think that Arnold's lovers could be so desperate and feel so alone in a world like ours. Here we were, you and I, two orphans, with no other family to speak of, and still we found our life together glorious. We did. Try to remember. Think of me here waiting for you. Think of the world as you knew it with me! We will be happy again, my darling, I promise you.

Well, then, he would take his endearments with medicine, he thought. But the pleas came to take over the letters, while the rest was reduced to abrupt, dutiful recountings of the health and carryings-on of her main characters.

Finding himself down to the last letter, he sighed deeply. There were two sheets, dated very shortly before the lieutenant's death. He thought he recognized the dirt smeared across the envelope. He turned to stare briefly through the coach window at the November greyness without, and then, instinctively pressing one hand against his chest, the sergeant read the letter.

My dearest Richard,

It has been an age since your last letter. If you are receiving mine—well, you must know what the silence does to increase my dread. I do not mean to burden you, but just a word or two would assure me that you are well.

This—this abject pleading is what I have been reduced to by your silence, and the strange tone of your last letter and the one before that. Those disturbing quotations. King Lear and Hamlet. Why send me sighs and lamentations from the stories of others, when what I want to know is how are <u>you</u>, my beautiful lad, my lieutenant? Write to me, my darling, <u>to</u> me and not around me.

I'm unusually tired tonight, my dear. The days grow short, and my ankle pains me. Oh, dear, scratch out that last bit. I know I've no right to complain. But I must make this brief for once. Please forgive me.

Little 'Becca died in the night Tuesday. I suspected it the next morning from the crape on the lea gate, and Alphaeus came to me that evening with the news. The wretched burial took place yesterday afternoon. Stonecroft accompanied the small coffin, his hand resting lightly on its cover, to the church by the beck, where she lies. He was almost destroyed by grief and spoke to me bitterly afterward about "the end of that poor abbreviated little story," which observation put a damp chill on all hearts present. He left his copse hermitage this morning without a word to anyone—for Calais, says the Sturgess, as she heard it from the stationmaster. And so that is for us the end of <u>his</u> story.

I miss you, my love. I shall be whole only when you return.

I kiss your eyes and lips.

Your Emma

Chapter 9

The sergeant woke at midday as the train pulled into a station and looked about him in confusion, afraid the conductor must have forgotten him until Berwick-upon-Tweed. But then he knew where he was and was grateful not to have slept through her stop. At first he thought he must have drifted off in mid-letter and arrived before he'd had a chance to finish. But then it came back to him, that last letter of hers. He had read it, rocking through the day in a compartment filled with evil oblique slants of light that flashed like distant artillery as the clouds surged past the sun. He remembered reading the letter, a strangled short one, and the moment of terrible vision returning—the lieutenant's silhouette pecking at the horizon against the night sky ("bark'd about all my smooth body, sergeant"). He had read the letter and lapsed into a trance of self-protection.

He collected the odd pages that had drifted off his knees when he'd been taken suddenly and helplessly by sleep. The old woman was gone. Two infantry Jocks, who must have entered the compartment while he slept, turned their heads from the spectacle of the sergeant gathering himself together. He stuffed the papers rudely into his pack. When the conductor came to alert him, he rose to leave the carriage.

"You're ham then, eh, sergeant?" asked one of the Scots.

"Yeh, lad."

"Lucky man," said the other.

"Yeh."

Pearce stumbled from the carriage onto the platform. A bitter wind slapped at his face. The letters weighed like a dead man on his back. Inside the tiny station house, he dropped onto a stool against a damp and weeping wall, trying to sort his thoughts, to suppress treacherous sobs, while the station master and his boy looked on curiously. When he thought he could bear it, he asked the way.

It was fiercely cold, but almost a broad day, as the hiccoughs of stinging wind shuddered away the clouds that had oppressed him since Southampton. The sky opened fair behind them. He lumbered forward in the direction which the wondering station master had indicated with a soft gesture, toward the squat line of cliffs that browed the shore.

It took two hours to reach the cottage and the low cliff overlooking a dreary stretch of sandy marsh to the sea. He was just barely aware of the odd cart and a sole motor passing, some few pedestrians. He waved away rides before they were offered. And when he'd gained the grey cottage, he looked seaward and thought that it was a moving prospect, but inhuman. The cottage itself appeared careworn: moss-invaded Northumbrian stone, timbers exposed and cracked in places. But she hadn't been in it long enough to make changes, he thought. If it was hers, in fact, if she could have brought herself to live here, overlooking the cold sand and the steely sea.

Hers was a double-hung door with no window and no bell. As he had before, reading her last letter, he pressed a fist against his chest, and when he reached for the knocker, the blood flew to his face and his hand shook. There was no answering voice, but the upper sash was drawn back, and there she was.

She looked so unexpected there. It wasn't that he was disappointed. She was just so unexpected—the reality of her, the solid, though narrow, shoulders, and the well of shadow along her collarbone.

Had she shone with an aura, he would have been less surprised, would have been relieved, in fact, to find her a spirit, an imagining, his own peculiar brand of shell shock, one that was gentle and deft at forgiving, not like those other ghosts he knew haunted the loonies, mates risen from the dead, disfigured and accusatory, climbing into windows and standing silently by beds as wives shook their men and worried, what is it, what is it this time? Not like the vision of the lieutenant searching for Sampson's foot. But she had none of the mythic about her, no hair entwined with flowers or fire in her eyes. And if she was real, shockingly real to him at the moment, still she had none of the lush or sensual either, no adorable peach skin or pouting mouth, forget-me-not blue eyes and soft yellow pleated blouse pulled over breasts that asked to be petted. She had none of that, either.

But she was a presence (he would have been daft to think otherwise), thin and stooped as she appeared in the low entrance, with shadowed eyes (grey-green, he thought) in a pale face and very dark hair, bobbed once but growing out now with an odd dash of silver, a streak along the front, to which her hand flew. She pushed the shining lock behind an ear. Her fingers were tinged with blue, and he thought briefly of mermaids.

And suddenly it was all he could do to take it in, all he could stand. The insistence of her cheated passion filled the space between them.

"Yes?" she asked. Her eyes touched his regiment, his rank, his pack, the shadow of a beard, the sunken eyes. "Richard's man? Your lieutenant's, I mean. My husband's."

"Yes."

She opened the bottom door then and turned, faltering (the ankle?), and motioned him in. The dress was black, of course, and plain, and she had draped a heavy knitted jacket, dark as well, across her narrow shoulders like a shawl. She was small-built and slender to an extreme, but her hip canted softly as she turned to him, and he pressed again on his heart.

"I'm sorry, I've not made up the fire today, but the sun seems to have warmed the sitting room in spite of the wind."

He tried to concentrate on what she was saying as he followed her inside, but it made no sense to him, that she would worry, could sound, in her lady's voice, somehow like all the women he knew at home ("worritin' 'bout t'coal, lad"). For the first time he wondered what her circumstances might be. The house was cold as corpses.

"But I've plenty of tea, so please sit down. You look very weary."

A soft lady's voice, with but a mite of Northumbrian Geordie. She haled from the place and was picking it up again, or had never lost it ("our moggie").

"I'd love a cuppa, missus. I'm that beat."

"Yes, I can see."

It took several seconds for his eyes to adjust to the low-beamed interior, penetrated by mere shards of light from deep-set windows in thick walls. He was concentrating on her form as it floated, it seemed to him, in spite of the ankle, across cold swept flags covered erratically by Turkey rugs in varying states of wear. She did not ring or call anyone (was there no Mrs. Lanton, no Audrey, or a local successor?), but left him sitting dumbly as she herself made tea for them out of sight in the kitchen. (He imagined her fine blue fingers turned rosy with warmth as she worked at the stove.) The furniture was largely what might be expected in such a place, the few stuffed pieces of faded yellows and greens, some with graphic figuring of a vaguely floral nature, repaired where the seams had burst. There were the serviceable rustic wooden bits—linen chest, occasional table, stepstool. A few oddities lurked in the shadows of the room in a way that accented their grotesqueness—a delicate antique secretary, an ornate china cabinet, its matching dining table secreted in the corner, two of its four chairs hung out of the way on hooks.

There was a single framed photograph. He had seated himself at angle from it and could not make it out.

Only two low-situated paraffin lamps were lighted (she'd taken another with her to the kitchen), though a few oil lamps and fewer candlesticks were spread about. The discolored glass chimneys gave the scene the paradoxical warmth and tawdriness of light shining through yellowed canvas—no, of a trench lantern swallowed by gassy mist.

He looked for something he could reference from her letters, but recognized nothing. Her home called up no sensations of intimate familiarity with her; it seemed irrelevant, accidentally interposing itself between him and her, or his idea of her.

Panic struck him obliquely, unexpectedly. He could smell the fear on himself. Who was the woman inhabiting this place? He'd stepped into the wrong world, as in a dream or story. (The giant would enter now and make a meal of him.) He'd made a terrible mistake, asked for too many wishes, or the wrong ones. He could not surrender his soul in such a place.

He would keep the letters for himself, then, cheated as he was of his heart's desire. He deserved them. They had survived, and he with them—not to be enshrouded in this place! He'd nursed them like a child in his breast while grinding bones beneath his feet and shattering bodies with his weapons. He'd fed on them with his terrible desire. He would cherish them as they deserved. She need never know.

He bolted forward at the sound of her step, though whether to assist her or flee, he hadn't decided when his eyes lighted on the arms of the loveseat opposite. In spite of a lot of greasy wear, they were free of antimacassars and paraded their wounds with a kind of stalwart petulance that was familiar after all. Touched, he met her coming from the kitchen and took the tea from her to the table beside the loveseat, and in so doing, saw the young man in the photograph. And so he sat where she motioned him, on the loveseat, and absently rubbed the already frayed arm with the thumb of his left hand while she poured for them.

"It's Sergeant Pearce, isn't it?" she asked with a smile, seating herself in an armchair. He felt his heart flop dangerously on hearing his name on her lips. "Richard wrote me, 'Our Sergeant Pearce is essential,'" she quoted, closing her eyes. " 'What does the subaltern do who must do without such a sergeant?' " She looked at him. He felt himself flush hard. He wished desperately to see her better than he was able in the poor light. "I know many of the men from their letters," she continued with forced conviviality, while he thought, *All of them—you know them all, except* . . . She rose from the chair and sat down beside him, looking into his face. "Have you anything for me?"

He shed his pack then, blushing to think he had kept it on his back all the while he sat accepting his tea. When he opened it to reveal the letters, no longer neatly tied with bits of string and laces, he caught a look at her face and felt himself transported, felt that something that had been missing was now restored. It wasn't a simple sensation, like the smell of dew on wet grass, or the slice of perfect light across the bed on his first marriage morning. It made no sense, the place he was transported to and the feeling it called up. For it was trenches again, muck and rot and human stench. The white ghosts of breath on the dense cold air. But it was also the snug knot of men and the letters, the lieutenant's wife, and the signal warmth of the faerie time and place she offered them. The heat of desire and the cool touch of her generosity. In this way, he found her again, for there was that expectation in her look as she awaited what he had for her, that same eagerness that all of them had shared once on her behalf, that same hanging on every word.

She dipped her thin hands into the lot and began examining them, and her brows knit in distress. "But they're all mine."

"Yes, mum," he said when he understood her. "He . . . was killed . . . before he had time to write another one."

"But he must have left something, told someone something . . . to tell me." Clusters of crushed letters in both hands. She dropped them and gripped his arm, throwing him into confusion. "I don't understand it. There must have been several, *many* letters that never got off because—because . . . I don't know why. You should know . . . I haven't heard, haven't had a line . . . for weeks, weeks before he died."

She was looking at him searchingly, and he had to look down. After a moment, she got up and he stood for her, miserably.

"I'm sorry, sergeant. I wondered what had happened, you see. Look. I'll show you." She went to the secretary then and extracted something from it, a small bundle of letters neatly tied with yellow silk. She took them to the sergeant. "The last one—on the top, I'd like you to read it please."

"Oh, missus, I shouldn't think you'd want—"

She was wringing her thin hands. "Please. Please. I want someone . . . I want *you* to know."

He tried not to feel awkward, standing too close to her, squinting to make out the lieutenant's hand in the bad light from shadowed east windows.

My dearest Emma,

Do you know the lines from Hamlet, my dear, about the garden gone to corruption, or the skin to bark, it is, but he means caked like clotted sores. Oh, God. Even this might do it—this small missive, this pilule, this blister of poison. I, for one, cannot bring it back, not to you or the silly bumbling beauties that surround you.

That was all. That and blots. He shook with the old horror—his lieutenant bobbing at the noxious earth, bobbing, bobbing for Sampson's foot. His face was wet, and he thought, hopelessly, it's too dark, isn't it? She can't see me crying, can she?

Then she had taken the letter from him and was looking at it. "I don't understand what he means—meant. I thought he enjoyed the letters. I wrote as long as I could after that. I wrote even after I lost heart—"

"He loved the letters. He told me so. They were everything to him. They were everything to all of us. They got us through, they did."

She was quiet.

"They were everything to him and to us, missus . . . mum," he repeated, and every hope of confessing himself to her dried to chaff in his throat.

Before he left her, he promised to contact her again, but she made no such promise herself—she never wrote letters now, she said. So for forty-one years he wrote to her without response, even from India, where he'd been posted in the next show and where he'd stayed on to help with the handover, once he'd admitted to himself, and Agnes had accepted, that he was regular army after all.

She never wrote, but she received visits, and it soon became clear to him that all of the men visited her from time to time, some yearly, some when they were in the area or needed the sight of her. They all made presents when they came, gifts of food, mostly, and small necessities; once in a while, a tanner or a bob hidden where she was sure to find it, but not until later, when she couldn't be certain it wasn't hers, after all. And they did the repairs, kept the cottage snug for her (because there would always be a question of her means). None of the lads would have found the words that deserted the sergeant—this he knew for certain.

She aged better than some of their wives and worse than others. She retained her presence, but lost her charm. They worshipped her to a man all the long years until one or another of the lads would die, meeting at last with the thing that had stalked them in trenches and which, for a while, she had cheated of them. And then, while there were still a few left to mourn her, she slipped away in the night.

He sometimes thought of her as the lieutenant's wife, sometimes as all of theirs, sometimes as his alone. He waxed hot on her memory some nights and grew moody over her remoteness on others. But all he took from her, and without her notice, was that first letter, the one with the postscript that had kept her man alive.

That day, on the threshold of her cottage, as he took his leave and she hugged herself in her black sleeves against the bitter wind, while he still hadn't realized he'd never hear of the vicar or the cook, the painter or the postmistress again, he brought himself to ask, "And the moggie, where is she?"

"Oh . . . . I gave her to Uttleys' dairy when I left. It seemed pointless, somehow, bringing her, when there are plenty of cats, you know, wherever one goes."

He looked past her into the house. "But you haven't a cat."

She paused. "No, I haven't."

He took her hand before turning away, and she kissed him on the cheek.

The walk back to the station along the remote cliff road seemed oddly full of people, as though the world had held its breath until he'd finished what he had begun. But of course, they were only a few really, no more than had been there earlier, walking or with their carts and bicycles, when he'd made his way toward the cliff that afternoon. He hadn't looked at them then, only wishing to see her in his mind. But now he didn't intend to let any of it slip by him—the busy life. Hell, he'd lost days already with Agnes waiting and wondering what on earth could be taking her man so long to come home.

Epilogue

We have found safety with all things undying,
The winds, and morning, tears of men and mirth,
The deep night, and birds singing, and clouds flying,
And sleep, and freedom, and the autumnal earth.
We have built a house that is not for Time's throwing.
We have gained a peace unshaken by pain for ever.
War knows no power. Safe shall be my going,
Secretly armed against all death's endeavour;
Safe though all safety's lost; safe where men fall;
And if these poor limbs die, safest of all.
--from "Safety," by Rupert Brooke

(Northumberland, 1950)

It was a bright spring day when Kate Worrall laid her eyes on the cottage on the cliff. She hadn't expected to find a cab in this poor spot ("na but a dog an' its flean," her mam would've said) and never intended to pay for one while she had her legs. But the eager young man and his ancient rattling Beardmore Mark-Something had touched her heart. "The Rolls-Royce of Taxis," he'd called it proudly, though it shook like St. Vitus and couldn't have much life left in it. He'd made her a bargain, hardly more than the petrol could have cost him to drive to the lonely spot.

The moment the tiny house became visible from the road, she told the lad drop her instead of leaving her at the door itself. She'd had the thought whilst settling herself for the bumpy ride that it wouldn't do to be pulling herself up out of the automobile, what with her bulk and all, when she arrived. She had her dignity, and it always seemed to her that she made a spectacle of herself leaving motor cars in this way, heaving her heavy legs before her and sometimes getting her skirt caught up to where she couldn't help giving anyone a peep of the top of her stockings. And though she was tired and felt old, and a mite guilty at deceiving her Tom, not that he hadn't done as much thirty-odd times in thirty years, it wouldn't do here to show garters, where there was a plain disadvantage in looking ridiculous before that one as lived in the cottage on the cliffs.

The Platoon's Whore, thought Kate, and saying it in her mind gave her strength, just as thinking of Agnes Pearce, fire-spitting Agnes, steeled her purpose. Add to that, she had the authority behind her of twelve living wives, as well as the dead ones, cheering her on, so she felt. But she reckoned that the best strategy, as she called it, was to pull herself up as tall and imposing as she could and stride to front door, on the chance the tart was watching from her windows.

It was like herself, though, she thought, to be distracted right off by the beauty of this day. She had lifted her chin (*chins*, her Annie would've said to provoke her) to sniff the sea air, and a blast of youthful joy struck her immediately. There was some of that pansy her mam called heart's ease, and hare bell, and a kind of flowering rocket and a tall plant with white clusters. Not in abundance, not too blousy or bold, mind you, but here and there on the wind-swept cliff-road, sheltering in nooks or against the low tumbled wall. She didn't like to turn from these fresh things to the task at hand. But, thankfully, the image of Agnes came to mind. Agnes had scolded her for weeping at what they had found out about the mystery in Northumberland. Agnes said they'd a right to be angry and no call to be crying. Agnes was a tough old bird; it was her as was the natural leader of their little rebellion, not Kate.

But, in spite of all that—Agnes's ire and Agnes's tongue—it had been decided that Kate Worrall would confront the woman, that she would come on behalf of herself and the rest of them. Agnes's temper alarmed some of the girls: she'd throw a fit at the very mention of the woman, badgering them all to show up in force and make a regular scandal in the tart's own village, until that one was forced to scarper someplace—France, maybe. (They'd all decided she was probably a French mistress the men had brought back with them. Calling herself by a common English name! Calling herself "Mrs" indeed!) Now, Kate, on the other hand, had that about her as was calming. It was true she'd been peacemaker in her mam's house since she could talk, and peacemaker in her own when Annie and the boys made a fuss. And she spoke higher than most of the other wives, though she couldn't have said where she got it, not having finished her schooling or even finished a book entirely before marrying her Tom and sending him off to the war.

It was Tom as came back from trenches hot on reading, and though it bored her stiff and made a distance between them, she knew it was Tom's fondness for his precious books as gave her kids the edge in school so that both of the lads ended up scholarship boys—their Bill a banker now in Lees, and their Neddie getting a schoolmaster position in Birmingham, and both of them would never see the inside of a coal pit. (Not that her boys were nancies, mind you: they'd a few lost teeth between them from defending themselves as boys and men.) She blushed remembering how she hadn't much patience with all of them reading all of the time like that.

And then when both the boys went for soldiers in '39 (and they'd got commissions for their educations, them!), she was heart-sore, and Tom wrote them almost every day, though paper was hard come by, and the Airgraph left little room for writing. He even used bits of butcher paper and the backs of bills. He insisted that he was doing his bit writing like that. "'T'will keep 'em safe, Katie girl," he told her. "Be summat ter live for." She'd been fierce with him over that, as if her and Annie and home and country weren't enough to live for but they had to have some bit of blethering every blessed day! But they'd come home safe, and she was ashamed how she'd nagged Tom, when after all, didn't she just feel like the odd one out most of the time? Even her Annie loved stories, making up tales, her, endless, fantastic things that could hold her brothers for hours, never mind she was just a girl and all.

(And then, truth be told, maybe it was this, her ignorance, that turned her Tom from her to that one in the cottage. Never a good old-fashioned prossie from round their village, but he had to go setting one up away up a cliff. What had she got that his Katie didn't, heh?)

But some of it, what her lads got from their books, must have rubbed off on Kate, as she found herself with the reputation for talking smart and for thinking straight and deep, though she didn't feel all that comfortable with the role herself.

The cottage itself didn't suggest anything she'd been feeling about the Platoon's Whore. It was as tidy as could be imagined, perched primly on the low cliff edge. She reached the double-sashed door, shook her head to clear away the temper and confusion, and knocked firmly.

When Kate emerged from that same doorway an hour later, she felt in her bag for a handkerchief, though once she had it in hand, she forgot whether she meant it to wipe a tear or hide a blush. So many letters! Drawers full of them! She'd been shown some from her Tom as made her redden, not because of anything they said, but because of what they didn't say—the foolish things she expected to read and burn over. Instead, they brought back her Tommy out of the fog of that past time, brought him to her mind as the boy he was going to war and then coming home crammed chock-a-block with those ideas of his—books and poetry, who'd have thought it?

And what didn't she know, then, the sweet lady, about Katie's own Bill and her Ned and their wives and kiddies ("bairns," she'd called them in the northern way)! And wasn't it a wonder her Tom could have told the lieutenant's wife so much about them all, when it was all Katie herself could do these days to get a word from him.

And now as she walked to that place in the road where she'd arranged to meet the taxi again, she was mithered she wouldn't know where to begin with them. For the platoon's secret had turned out to be none other than the lieutenant's wife, a gentle wraith in black wool jumper and skirt, hollow-eyed and frail (not enough there to make it worth a man's heartbeat) and old, older than Kate had thought, her imagining of the Platoon's Whore not having kept pace with her own aging.

"I am Kate Worrall!" she had said smartly, keeping the shake out of her voice, when the sash was drawn back, "Tom Worrall's missus!" And the lieutenant's wife had opened the lower door and gathered Kate into her arms, as if Kate, all twelve stone of her, was no more than a child. Astonished, Kate had peered over the woman's shoulder at a photograph she recognized, and, realizing her mistake, years of mistake, babbled something about coming on behalf of the wives, the remaining wives, to remember the lieutenant their men had loved.

And so Kate left the cottage an hour later with what letters the two of them could gather as had the names of the men still living on them. It was her penance for mistrusting her Tom that now she would have to explain to the rest of the Platoon wives that there'd been no carryings-on after all, that they'd made a mistake and almost acted the fool. It was a mistake easily made, mind you: it was a common name, the commonest, now she came to think of it, common-sounding, too, since Kate knew many of her own class (or lower) as had that name, spelt different sometimes, it was true. So even if she hadn't recognized the lieutenant from his photograph what was also the one from the clipping her sister had sent her, even if the two names hadn't clicked, it was a mistake easily made. One thing was clear, though: it wasn't *her* fault, her as lived in that cottage, their lieutenant's wife. She'd welcomed Kate and fed her tea. She hadn't known what they were all thinking about her. Lord, it was a good thing that it was Kate there after all and not that hot-headed Agnes Pearce!

And it was a weight lifted, she thought, to know her Tommy wasn't dipping his wick here regular, when he'd a wife back home who loved him, though why the whole thing had been kept such a bloody great secret was a question she didn't care to think on. Never mind now, she thought. It was enough to know how good they'd all been, those lads, to the lieutenant's wife, for the lieutenant's sake, of course. And she wouldn't forget, not ever, how the woman held her two large hands, what felt like fat puddings in those two thin ones, and said, "Those lads, those wonderful lads. They've kept me alive these last thirty years. They made it possible to live."

It was embarrassing, almost, this lady, an officer's wife, blinking back the tears like that, though it all seemed natural at the time, and anyway, she could use them—them tears—to make the others pity the woman and drop it. And they must never mention it to their men, please God! She couldn't ask the woman to keep mum about her own visit, and Tom would be sure to find out. Any road up, it didn't matter. He *should* know, though she'd never bring it up herself, and knowing it together like that would make them closer, for now she thought of it, it had only been this really, this secret, that stood between them all those years.

Finally, she heard the shuddering engine of the old Beardmore, as the taxi made its way to her, must be at least twenty minutes past the time they'd agreed on. Well, never mind, it was a beautiful day, and when a sudden gust of wind picked up her skirt, she felt lighter than she had in years.

ACKNOWLEDGEMENTS

Thank you to William Lawrence, my publisher and editor, for inviting me into the family of Serving House authors.

This book quite literally would not exist without Barbara Froman. Thank you for this, Barb, and for our many glorious years of wonderful camaraderie.

I am fortunate to have many writers as friends; without them my work wouldn't be what it is and my life wouldn't be as full.

I am especially indebted to Ellen Wade Beals, Ellen McKnight, Paula Peterson, Barb Shoup, Judy Smith and Beth Wetmore, who dedicated more time and counsel to these stories than a reasonable person could hope to receive. Your input has been crucial, but never more essential than your friendship.

I'm honored to have been part of the writing groups that, while encouraging my evolution as a writer, became my cherished community. To the Writers of Glencoe (IL) and to the members of "Marvin's Group," I'm grateful to you all.

For believing in me all these years, my heartfelt thanks go to Charlotte DiGregorio, Terry Fucik, Lora Gettleman and my beloved sister Nancy Megan Corwin.

The only beings who have given more and suffered more on behalf of my writing are my husband and children. My gratitude and love for you are infinite.

FIRST PUBLICATION CREDITS

"Details," in *Solace in So Many Words*, ed. Ellen Wade Beals (Hourglass Books, 2011).

"Girls With Guns," *Sycamore Review* 24.2 (Summer/Fall, 2012).

"Hindsight," *River Oak Review* 20 (Spring/Summer, 2003).

An excerpt was included in the anthology *(AFTER)life: Poems and Stories of the Dead*, eds. Renée M. Schell, Barbara Froman and Marta Svea Wallien, (Purple Passion Press, 2015).

"Point Man," *Crate* 5 (2009).

Safe Shall Be My Going, in the *Press 53 Open Awards Anthology*, eds. Sheryl Monks and Kevin Watson (Press 53, 2008).

"Settling Accounts," *Inkwell* 28 (Fall, 2010).

"Wings," *Roanoke Review* 33 (Spring, 2008).

ABOUT THE AUTHOR

Before turning to full-time fiction writing, Joan Corwin taught literature and Victorian social history at Chicago-area colleges and universities. She has received several writing awards, among them, the Dana Portfolio Award, the Press 53 Open Award (Novella category), the Chris O'Malley Prize in Fiction and the Tom Howard/John H. Reid Fiction Prize. Her short story *Hindsight* was a Chicago Public Radio "Stories on Stage" winner. Her fiction has appeared in a number of literary journals such as *StoryQuarterly, Sycamore Review* and *The Madison Review*, as well as the anthologies *Falling Backwards: Stories of Fathers and Daughters; Solace in So Many Words; (AFTER)life: Poems and Stories of the Dead*, and *Signs of Life: Contemporary Jewelry Art & Literature*. She lives in the Chicago area with her husband and their two dogs.

www.ingramcontent.com/pod-product-compliance
Lightning Source LLC
Chambersburg PA
CBHW032223190726
48289CB00007BA/2367